SHAKIRAN

LARISSA'S STORY

SUSAN McKENZIE

ReamStories subscription:
https://reamstories.com/susanmckenzie
Amazon author page:
amazon.com/author/susancarter
Visit Sue's website:
http://susanmckenzieauthor.com
Follow Sue on Facebook:
https://www.facebook.com/SueMcKenzieAuthor

YOUR FREE BOOK IS WAITING

The novelette

THE ALIEN

is free for a limited time. You just need to tell me where
to send it

When Lilliana crash-lands her spaceship on a Primitive
planet, she'll have to rely on help from an attractive
local to survive.

**Use the QR Code to follow the link, then enter your name
and email address to get your free book delivered to your
inbox**

Or type this link into your browser: https://www.subscri
bepage.com/thealien

WHAT READERS LIKE YOU ARE SAYING...

"Shakiran: Larissa's Story by Susan McKenzie is an amazing story to read. I loved reading this story very much I don't usually like Sci-Fi much but I was hooked on this story from the beginning. I highly recommend this story to everyone who loves reading about Sci-Fi and paranormal romance."
  — Scarolet Ellis (Amazon Review)

"I really enjoyed this book. I found the characters to be interesting and I think what made them interesting is that they weren't perfect and that just made them more relatable. The story is well thought out and the author has done a great job in the execution."
  — Annie555 (Amazon Review)

"I love it... I thought it was awesome... I cried along with Larissa."
  — Kimberly Rodighiero (Early Reader)

To my sister, Debbie.

No matter what life throws at us, you will always be my big sister that I had so much fun singing ABBA songs with when we were kids. I love you.

CHAPTER 1

I Thought You Shakirans Were All Bloodthirsty Warriors

Concentrating on what someone was saying wasn't usually this hard.

Focus, Larissa.

They'd given each of us a Palm-pad to take notes on, so I thought I'd better take notes, or at least look like I was.

The presenter droned on about the natives of the planet we would be studying, but this wasn't new information. Everything he'd said so far was in the reports I'd received after being accepted for the job at Voyager Division. But I wouldn't be studying the natives. My job revolved around the plant life and Althar 3 was teeming with it.

I needed to get up and walk around the room. If I sat here any longer, his monotone voice would put me to sleep.

The only interesting thing in the room was the Shakiran sitting on the opposite side of the table and to my right. It was hard to keep my eyes from drifting back to him. White-blonde hair almost as long as my own, and those piercing dark eyes. With so many people from different planets here on the space station, another Shakiran stood out. Our height difference was one of the main reasons, being head and shoulders above the average race.

The only other person here that was as tall was the Ziflarian sitting to my left. She was amazingly beautiful with her dark skin and long, black, curly hair flowing over her shoulders. Most Shakirans had fair skin and blonde hair, so our races were polar opposites when it came to colour.

I looked around at the other new employees of the Voyager Division and my eyes found the Shakiran's again. He was looking straight at me, his brown eyes almost black. I quickly looked away and tried to concentrate on the presentation.

My heart rate picked up. He'd been stealing glances at me the whole time. I assumed it was because we were both Shakiran, but maybe there was more to it. I hoped there wasn't because I was here to work, not socialise, and that meant no relationships.

At all.

I didn't want all the hassles that came with it.

I tried to see what he was doing by keeping him in my peripheral vision and he was staring at me. Again.

I wanted to look, but I managed to keep my attention on the blue eyes of the presenter, who stopped abruptly and announced that we would be going around the room introducing ourselves to the group. I took a deep breath. I would find out his name.

Stop it.

We were sitting at a long table with three people on each side and one sitting at the end.

The presenter, Fenrick, looked at the woman to his left. She sat on the opposite side of the table from me, but to my left. She was short and had shoulder-length sandy-brown hair and excitement flashing in those blue eyes.

She cleared her throat. "I'm Zhenna Rhodarma and I'm a computer programmer from Earth. I've never been off-world so

I thought I'd sign up to see the universe and I will do what I can to keep the computers running smoothly at Station Jannali."

The presenter smiled warmly. "Thank you, Zhenna." He turned to the man to her right. "Next?"

The man was taller than Zhenna and had a rugged appearance and broad shoulders. "I am Mosuti Kyah. I'm a Linguist from the planet Moftar. I have extensive experience in first-contact liaisons with new races."

The presenter raised his eyebrows. "You're the Talent sent to study the Altharian languages, yes?"

"That's correct."

"Hmm. Fascinating." He looked to the Shakiran. "And you are?"

"Janssen Malakua. I'm a botanist from the planet Shakira." *A botanist?* I sucked in a breath and his eyes darted to me as he continued. "I aim to study many different plant species in the universe in order to take that information back to Shakira to improve the crops we grow in my family's business. In the meantime, my priority is to offer my expertise to your company."

A botanist. What were the chances of two people from Shakira applying for jobs as botanists on a planet out on the edge of the Known Universe at the same time? Especially since Shakirans usually choose careers in the military.

His eyes met mine again and I closed my mouth and looked away. I'd been staring too long.

"Very good. Yes," Fenrick said. He turned to the portly man at the end of the table. "Yes?"

"The name is Kami Olion. I'm a sociologist from Setlur. I offer my services to you, but I have some questions."

"Mmm-hmm. Yes?"

"Will we be expected to go out into the jungle? I mean, I have my health to consider. There would be diseases that we aren't immune to and then there's the dangers of the wildlife—"

"Don't worry, Mister Olion. Your position will involve indoor work only. It's in the job description and in your contract."

"Hmm. Well. Yes. I was just clarifying this before I fully committed myself. You understand?"

Fenrick nodded. "Yes, I understand. But you do understand that you have already signed the contract, thereby fully committing yourself to this position, yes?" When Kami didn't answer, he looked to the man next to me. "Now to our next candidate—"

"And there's also the question of the two week's travel," Kami said. "Surely the company can use a better class of ship to get us there faster than that?"

Fenrick pursed his lips. "Voyager Division is paying for your tickets and providing you with accommodation and all meals aboard the ship, sir, so I'm sure you will be—"

"Voyager Division is a large company. Surely they can afford a faster ship."

He sighed. "Mister Olion, the Acronis is a well-equipped Class IV cruiser and it is the ship the company uses. If you have a problem with it, I suggest you take it up with my superiors. I am merely here to give you the information you will need before you set off for Althar 3."

Kami grumbled under his breath for a while.

A person who complained about everything and behaved like a child was without honour or integrity.

Fenrick looked again at the man on my right. "I'm sorry. Please continue."

This man was probably the shortest person in the room, but his eyes were bright and alert. "Hey everyone, I'm Lanu Ricksha. I'm a sociologist from Vanitha. I'm so excited to be joining you all on this journey and to be studying newly-discovered races."

Fenrick smiled and I could see he was as relieved as I was that he was nothing like Kami. "Thank you, Lanu." He smiled at me and nodded.

I sat a little straighter. "I'm Larissa Malinya. I'm a botanist, also from Shakira." Now it was Janssen who sucked in a breath. "I'm interested in the use of plants for their medicinal qualities and look forward to studying the new plant species on Althar 3."

Kami turned to me. "I thought you Shakirans were all bloodthirsty warriors and here we have two of you who are plant lovers."

CHAPTER 2
I Meant No Dishonour

My fists clenched and I glared at him. "We are not *blood-thirsty*. Do not make assumptions."

Janssen's eyes were fire. "You understand that a society cannot function without food, yes? Other professions are needed."

Fenrick spread his arms wide. "Now, let's calm down here. Let's channel peace. I will ask Mister Olion to refrain from making any derogatory comments about fellow workers. It's part of company policy, which forms part of the contract you have signed."

Kami mumbled under his breath again, but didn't say anything more.

I hoped that he decided to cancel his contract so he wouldn't be going with us.

Fenrick turned to the Ziflarian. "Please go ahead, dear."

She smiled and looked around the room. "Hi. I am Bazeelia Shamari and I am a scientist from the planet Ziflar. I am looking forward to working with you all. The discoveries we will make together will be awesome."

A scientist. I smiled. It fit her well.

I looked around the table. We had a mixed bag from across the universe, which would make things interesting.

I tried to imagine us working together as a group. I'd spent my whole life surrounded mostly by Shakirans and the occasional alien, and my grandmother was Taonese, but to see so many diverse races in the same room was different. And *exciting*.

Most Shakirans had a very narrow view of the universe and our history was marred by many wars with other races on nearby planets, but with my grandmother being from Taon, I had a somewhat wider view than other Shakirans.

I was looking forward to this job. I would be able to observe people from so many places — without getting personally involved with their lives — while learning as much as I could about the flora on the planet.

I had to remind myself that I was here to work, not to make friends.

My heart grew heavy. This wasn't what I'd originally planned to do after my graduation. Things changed in an instant as soon as the news of my grandmother's death had come through to the university. I needed to get away from my life for a while and get over losing the last member of my family. I needed to somehow heal my broken heart and move on with Gran's plan to use plants to heal instead of the usual Shakiran way of war and death.

I tried to smile. This would be a perfect distraction until I had my emotions under control and my head sorted out. Once my contract was up, I would put all my efforts into finding new uses for my plants and healing as many people as I possibly could. I couldn't get rid of my heartache, but maybe I could prevent someone else's.

I waited impatiently near the airlock of the shuttle that had taken us from the Acronis down to the surface of Althar 3. After two long weeks aboard the Acronis, I needed to get out. I wanted fresh air and to see the sun.

Where is everyone? Don't they want to see this?

The shuttle, the Outrider, had developed a mechanical fault, forcing us to land for immediate repairs before we could reach Station Jannali, the underground base we would be working from. We'd had to land in a tropical jungle.

An *actual* jungle.

And we were going outside to see it first-hand.

Sure, we had forests near my house on my home planet of Shakira, but this was nature at its wildest.

I could hardly stand still. I'd studied botany for the last two years, so to see the plant life on a newly-discovered planet would be exciting. I'd seen the reports and photos of course, but nothing would compare to the real thing. Up till now I'd only ever had the chance to study plant specimens from my home planet of Shakira and a select few from Earth.

Excitement buzzed through my veins.

Where are they?

I resisted the urge to start pacing.

Of course the rest of the crew wouldn't be as excited as I was to see the wild flora just outside these doors... But there was one person. The only other botanist on the ship. The only other Shakiran on the ship.

As if fate had heard my thoughts, Janssen rounded the corner and stopped in his tracks as my heart stuttered to a halt.

His dark eyes widened as they found mine. "Larissa. Hi." He inclined his head.

I returned the nod. "Hello."

Please don't ask about last night.

His eyes never left mine. "Can I talk to you?"

No. Not now. I can't talk to you now. Maybe not ever. "Uh, we don't have time." I looked both ways down the corridor. "Everyone will be here shortly..."

He looked around to make sure we were alone and lowered his voice. "*Please*. I need to know what I did to upset you."

My chest tightened. "Nothing. You did nothing wrong."

"Then why did you run off?"

"I—" *I can't tell you.* I took a deep breath. "It's not you. It's... something I can't talk about right now."

"I'm sorry if I was too forward, or if my kiss offended you, but you seemed to be responding..." He looked like he was in pain. "I meant no dishonour."

"I..."

He ran a hand through his long hair. "Why won't you talk to me? Is there something you're not telling me?" His eyes widened. "Are you betrothed?"

I cringed. "No."

"Are you — have you formed a union with someone? Have you lied to me these past weeks?"

"No!"

"Please don't dishonour me. If that's what it is—"

"It's nothing like that. There's no one. I—"

Voices and footsteps abruptly ended our conversation and I saw the hurt in his eyes as the room filled with people.

Guilt wrapped itself around my chest and squeezed. "We'll talk. Later."

He gave me a sad smile that I could easily see over everyone's heads. I turned away so I couldn't see his handsome face. I should never have become close to him. I should have kept my distance during our journey.

No relationships. No entanglements.

Why couldn't I stick to my plan?

The shuttle's pilot made his way through the small crowd and stood in front of the airlock doors. He reminded us that the air was breathable and ran through the procedures for exiting through the airlock — and what we were required to do once we were outside.

Once he'd reported that we had no choice but to land, one of the scientists at Station Jannali had suggested we make ourselves useful and collect some plant and soil samples. I'd opted for a plant sample — naturally — and they'd given me the job of finding a type of fungi called Aatrox.

As the pilot spoke, images of the prehistoric wildlife I'd seen in the reports played in my mind on repeat. It had me a little nervous. There were some dangerous creatures here. Even dangerous plants. We needed to be vigilant.

We stepped into the airlock and it sealed itself. Once it had finished depressurizing, the outer doors opened with a hiss and sunlight poured in through the gap in the canopy high above. My heart pounded. We'd landed in a small clearing caused by a fallen tree. A few of my fellow crew members filed out ahead of me and I padded down the ramp to the jungle floor. Humidity closed in around me in total contrast to the cool interior of the shuttle.

We stood gaping at the giant trees that formed the canopy. They were covered with moss and had vines intricately woven around their trunks and branches. The small creatures jumping around in the higher branches looked like monkeys. Birds flitted through the treetops and swooped down toward the ground.

The smaller trees boasted many shades of green. The wide variety of fungi growing on rocks and tree trunks displayed so many colours that they rivalled the countless flowers.

Some of the aromas from the flowers were almost familiar and one definitely smelled like an Airlea Blossom. The scent of nutrient-rich soil was hard to ignore and was so welcome after the sterile air we'd breathed for the last two weeks.

The undergrowth was so thick here and I wondered how any of the larger animals could find their way through. It was fascinating to see how plants formed when they were left to their own devices.

I closed my eyes and listened to the sounds of birds, crickets, and frogs, but I was startled by the sound of flapping wings high above us. Something scurried amongst the underbrush to my right. This was no time to be closing my eyes. Images of the many carnivorous dinosaurs and huge cat-like predators that inhabited this jungle flashed in my mind again. We were vulnerable out here in the open. We were not armed. If we were attacked, there would be no way to defend ourselves.

Surely our new employer wasn't stupid enough to send us out of the ship and leave us defenceless.

I looked to the people around me. At how unprepared and clueless they were.

Yes, they *were* that stupid.

I searched for any possible threats and noticed Janssen was on high alert too. Our combat training had been instilled in us from an early age and was impossible to switch off. Shakirans prided themselves on being a warrior race and all citizens were trained in the art of combat. No exceptions.

Being thrust into the jungle unarmed on the first day didn't sit well with me.

Our eyes met and Janssen nodded. We'd been thinking the same thing, but guilt over last night had me turning away.

People started to spread out toward the edges of the clearing and I remembered we had a job to do.

I squared my shoulders and headed for the nearest fallen log. The information contained in the PocketPC I'd been given said that the Aatrox was purple and grew on the underside of logs, but I planned to approach each log with a great deal of caution. Any number of creatures could be sheltering underneath.

Bazeelia strode purposefully toward some red flowers, her long black hair swishing back and forth from its ponytail. It seemed she'd found her target already.

She pulled out a sample case and a pair of clippers. She would be finished in no time and I hadn't even started.

The thunderous sound of flapping wings drew my attention and a huge winged reptile swooped down from the trees. Its screech hurt my ears and I instinctively ducked and screamed.

Bazeelia's scream was comical and mine was embarrassing. I *never* screamed.

Eli would've scowled at me for being such a coward...

I clenched my jaw. I couldn't be thinking about him now.

Janssen and Lanu had both given a shout when the reptile swooped, but were now laughing at us.

Bazeelia scowled. "Don't be laughin' at me. That thing was a monster! And it scared you too!"

Janssen turned to her, his hair falling fluidly over his shoulder as he moved. "Hey. Take it easy. We're just messin' with ya."

That may have been true, but she was right. Its wing-span was about three metres and its long, pointed beak was full of razor-sharp teeth.

Lanu strode over, smiling as he approached. "You've got to admit it was amazing though."

Bazeelia glared down at him, her mouth hanging open. "Amazing? No. It wasn't. It was terrifying!"

Lanu kept smiling, and I recognised that look of awe on his face. I had a photo of me back at home, taken after I'd created a new plant species in our nursery, and my face had that same look. That same light shone in my eyes.

He rubbed his chin. "But that thing is so similar to the Pteranodon from Earth's past and it flew within a few metres of us. It's like going back to the Cretaceous Period and getting a first-hand look."

"Well, you can go look at it and admire its beauty if you want. Pat it. Study it. Although I'm not sure being a sociologist will help when it comes to dinosaurs. Me? I'm glad I'll be working indoors once we get to Jannali." She flipped her long hair over her shoulder and went back to retrieving the red flower.

The fact that we weren't going to be interacting with the natives while we were here probably meant this would be our first and only time in the jungle. Maybe that was why they were okay with us being out here now. We were getting a taste of the environment these people lived in.

It was still dangerous out here; we needed to finish quickly and return to the safety of the ship.

I continued to monitor our surroundings.

Kami, who had continued to be a nuisance to us all since our first briefing, called from the doorway of the shuttle, asking Zhenna what the screaming was about. As she explained what had happened, I tried to ignore the conversation so I could get back to my search for the fungi. Kami had refused to come outside, saying the mechanical failure was a bad omen or some such nonsense.

He told her again that we should have stayed in the ship and kept insisting that Zhenna go back inside. What was his reason for only inviting her? That was odd. And it got my attention.

Zhenna and I had become friends on the trip out here, although I'd kept a certain distance between us.

I wandered over, feeling the need to protect her. If she agreed to go back in, I was ready to stop her. I did *not* trust the man. He was from Setlur, so there was a natural distrust for his whole race — Shakira had been at war with Setlur about two hundred years ago. Kami had shown his dislike for Janssen and I openly from the start, but there was more to my distrust of him than our races' shared history. His behaviour was suspicious and I wanted to keep Zhenna safe.

"Umm, I can't," she told him, the sunlight making her hair look almost blonde. "Jannali wants the samples. It's going to give a bad impression if we refuse."

I was relieved that she was staying out here.

His bushy eyebrows drew downward and his mouth became a straight line, but then he turned quickly and went back into the ship.

Good.

"Don't worry about him," I said as I reached her side. "He's just a superstitious old grump." *And a creepy old man.*

Old was a bit of a stretch. He was probably about thirty, but he acted like my grandfather.

She laughed at that, then cringed.

I shrugged. "I don't care if he hears me."

She giggled.

Zhenna was one of the few people I'd gotten to know on my way out here and although she had no interest in botany, we shared an interest in art and music. She was easy to talk to and it made me forget that I was only out here for work, not to socialise. She made it easy to get distracted from my goal, and so did Janssen. He'd been a *big* distraction.

I pushed those thoughts aside. I had a job to do.

We turned our attention back to the edge of the clearing so we could get the samples before the pilot finished with the repairs. I didn't want to turn up to Jannali empty-handed. How would that look? *"You're a botanist and you couldn't find a plant?"*

No. That wouldn't do. I would not shame myself.

I chose another log over where Zhenna was standing and headed straight to it, but my attention was drawn to Janssen's voice, as it often was. I couldn't help myself. He was reaching up to a low-hanging vine, and I tried to guess what his target was — the moss or fungi growing on the vine, or the vine itself?

I scolded myself for watching him and took another step toward the log. Every time he spoke, I looked over. What was wrong with me? I needed to exercise some self-control.

He caught me looking and my cheeks flushed. I needed to stop this and get back to work.

I checked to see if Zhenna had seen me; she was watching me and smiling. Those blue eyes missed nothing.

She pursed her lips as she tried not to laugh. "I saw you looking at him."

CHAPTER 3
Stay Down!

Dammit. "No, I wasn't."

She raised an eyebrow.

My cheeks heated even more. "Okay. I was."

When I looked back, the vine was hanging down lower and Janssen ducked under it, his long hair falling over his broad shoulder.

"You like him," she said.

The jungle suddenly seemed a lot warmer. She didn't know the half of it. "I... Uh... maybe. I don't know."

I couldn't tell her the truth.

"Well, you'll have plenty of time to find out since you'll be working together."

And that was the problem I was trying to ignore. Janssen and I would be studying the flora of this planet together while I tried to pretend I didn't have feelings for him.

How was I going to do that?

Getting to know him had been a mistake. I wasn't supposed to get close to anyone out here. Relationships led to heartbreak. I needed to keep away from him.

Somehow.

After checking our surroundings for any movement in the jungle, I watched him pack his sampling gear away and crouch down to look at a lavender flower. "Is he unattached, do you know?"

Why did I ask that? What is wrong with me?

Of course, I knew the answer to that question only too well.

"It has taken you two weeks to even ask that?" Her mouth hung open and she quickly closed it. "I heard him telling Mosuti he doesn't have a girl. Or boy."

I sighed and tried to look relieved and she chuckled.

I wasn't sure why I didn't want anyone to know how well Janssen and I knew each other. Maybe because I was ashamed at how easily I'd broken my own no-relationship rule. We'd met in the ship's hydroponics garden every night after everyone else was asleep where we talked about life in general and our interest in plants. And then last night things changed. He'd kissed me. And I'd kissed him back.

And then I'd run out on him.

Mosuti approached us, sweat from the humidity causing his dark curls to stick to his forehead. "Hey, girls."

"Hey," we answered in unison.

Mosuti's head reached my shoulder and Zhenna's only came to halfway up my upper arm. I was still trying to get used to the fact that most people I'd met since leaving Shakira were so short.

Mosuti smiled. "Found your specimens yet?"

We both said "no" at the same time and laughed. He was the one with the gift of telepathy and Zhenna and I were sounding like we were able to read each other's minds.

I glanced around the area and into the jungle again.

Zhenna looked toward the shuttle and I followed her gaze. Kami's stocky frame filled the doorway again. She kept her eyes on him as she whispered, "Mosuti. Kami doesn't like you, does he?"

Mosuti frowned. "I'm afraid not, Zhenna. Says he doesn't like my 'kind.'"

She glared at Kami. "Don't let it worry you. He's a douchebag."

Mosuti remained calm. "He doesn't worry me."

Kami called out again in his whiny voice. "Zhenna, dear, why are you talking to *him?*"

She shifted her feet in the leaf litter. "Uh, because he's my *friend.*"

"His kind can't be trusted. He's probably reading our minds right now."

Mosuti squared his shoulders. "I would *never* do that. It is against the Talents' Code of Conduct to read a being's mind without consent."

The Code of Conduct was put in place to protect people from telepathic intrusion and to protect the rights of the Talents themselves. It was a well-known fact. One that Kami would have knowledge of. He was just being difficult.

Why did he have to continually stir up trouble? He was such a bigot. He'd taken every opportunity over the last two weeks to argue with everyone and complain about the food and the conditions aboard the ship. He was disrespectful and self-absorbed.

I stepped toward him, fists clenched at my sides. "You're a jerk! What would you know about Talents? You're so narrow-minded!"

He dismissed me with a wave of his hand. "They are nothing but freaks. Mutated beings that taint our genetics."

Zhenna took a deep breath. "What do you suggest we do with these 'mutants'?"

He didn't waver. "We need to keep them under control. They shouldn't be allowed to wander free where they can manipulate our minds and wreak havoc across the universe."

"So, we should enslave them?"

"I... wouldn't use that exact term... but what else can we do? They're freaks of nature and they are a danger to us all."

This man had no honour. Someone needed to put him in his place. I looked to Mosuti, who seemed unaffected. He was probably used to such ignorance.

Mosuti's voice floated into my mind. *"It's okay. Don't worry about me. I'm fine."*

I gave him a nod and thought, *As you wish.*

On the trip out here, he'd shown me how to hold a telepathic conversation with him without possessing any Talent so I knew that he was able to read my response from my mind.

As long as he was okay, I would try to ignore this insult, not only to Mosuti, but to all Talents throughout the Known Universe.

Zhenna clenched her fists. She wasn't willing to let it go. "I'm glad I won't be working with you when we get to Jannali. You're such an arrogant, narrow-minded, backwards hick!"

I stifled a laugh.

Kami didn't get the chance to respond before laser fire burst through the jungle. I ducked my head instinctively, confused as to where it could be coming from.

"What was that?" Zhenna squeaked as she looked around wildly.

Mosuti threw us to the ground by way of an answer. "Stay down!" he ordered.

There was more laser fire and screaming. Guilt sliced through me when I realised I hadn't kept an eye on the jungle.

"Laser fire," I heard Mosuti whisper between shots. He'd landed facing Zhenna so I couldn't see their faces.

Another scream. Zhenna popped her head up, but quickly ducked back down, no doubt realising how foolish that move was.

I couldn't see much from my position, but movement caught my eye. Someone ran through the trees toward the shuttle. I didn't know who it was, but he didn't have long blonde hair. Pain sliced through my chest. What if Janssen was hit? What if he—

No. I couldn't go there. I couldn't lose another person I cared about. Not so soon after losing Gran.

I squeezed my eyes shut. I would not cry. I would not give in to my emotions right now. That would *not* help me. I needed to think. Who would be using laser weapons in the middle of a prehistoric jungle out on the edge of the Known Universe? Surely these primitives wouldn't have enemies who possessed advanced technology. That could only mean we were the target.

Who would want to attack us? We were just a group of scientists. It didn't make sense. Maybe it was another company that wanted to study these natives or take the planet's resources for themselves.

Surely they would go about it another way.

Or maybe they were a group of space pirates out for spoils. We had nothing of value besides the ship itself — a small shuttle used to ferry us from the Acronis to the surface. There was nothing on board worth the risks they were taking.

My attention was drawn to my hand, where a large beetle was making its way along my finger. I resisted the urge to flick it away. I needed to stay still.

My eyes darted around. The leaf litter teemed with life. A few more beetles and some ants crawled on me and there was something on Mosuti's arm. There were more crawling things on my legs and something on my shoulder. They didn't worry me too much; I'd been working in gardens since I was seven. I tried not to think about them crawling on me. As long as I kept still, I probably wouldn't get bitten. Maybe.

Another scream.

I tried to calm my breathing, but hearing more shots being fired all around us made it difficult.

All went quiet, but that wasn't necessarily a good thing. I waited for their next move.

The others lay with me on the ground, waiting, listening. Footsteps came closer and stopped. "These ones are good..."

I sucked in a breath. Slowly. Quietly. *Good for what?*

"Don't damage them," said another.

My blood ran cold thinking about what that could mean. My body tensed, waiting for a blow or the burn of a laser pistol. After all my efforts to avoid joining the armed forces back home, it seemed I was about to die at the hands of a gun anyway. How pathetically ironic.

Pain ripped through me and my body convulsed. The world faded to black.

CHAPTER 4
You Are Lucky to Be Alive

I knew immediately that something wasn't right. My muscles were stiff and sore and my head pounded. Why did I feel so bad?

I opened my eyes to a dark room and tried to remember what I'd done before I'd gone to sleep. My mind searched for a clue.

We'd been travelling through space for a fortnight... we'd landed... the jungle... laser fire—

Now I was fully awake. My heartbeat raced and my head pounded faster to match.

I knew what I was feeling. Why I felt so bad. I knew I'd been hit with a stunner.

In combat training at school, we'd been shown what it feels like to be shot with a stun gun. Yes, on Shakira, they actually shoot their twelve-year-olds with stunners. It was totally normal and totally acceptable. It was a necessary part of our education. So we were told.

I knew I'd feel this way for the next few hours, at least. It depended on the strength of the stunner blast.

I tried not to think about that. I needed to assess the situation. Where was I? Who attacked us? What did they want? Was I a prisoner? Had someone from Voyager Division stepped in and saved us?

I was in a soft bed in a small room with a tiny singular light on the ceiling that barely illuminated the walls.

A humming noise startled me, but I breathed a sigh of relief when I recognised the dark shadow of a Bio-scan floating past and scanning me from my head down to my feet. Once it scanned my vitals, it returned to its resting place at the head of the bed. I was most likely in a medical facility.

Once it landed, I stretched and sat up, putting my bare feet out onto a cold floor. Where were my shoes? I ran my hands over my clothing and through my hair. The small braids and beads I liked to put in my hair had been taken out and my clothes were different. A chill ran down my spine. Someone had changed my clothing while I was out.

My heart was trying to beat its way out of my ribcage, but I refused to let my fear rule my actions. I took a deep breath and let it out slowly. I needed to find out what was going on, and fast.

I could make out a door to my left, so I crept over and tried to activate the lock, with no luck. Maybe I *was* a prisoner.

My headache increased and I attempted to slow my breathing, but it was difficult. I needed to stay calm and think. Panicking now would not help me.

Maybe there were cameras in the room. Maybe they knew I was awake and I could get some answers.

It was too dark to see much of anything. I walked around a little to try to work out the stiffness in my legs. Moving my arms hurt too, but I pushed through it. A stunner blast caused every muscle to contract, so you were left feeling like you'd had an intense muscle cramp. All over.

The sooner my muscles were back to normal, the better. Not only because I would feel better, but I needed to be in a position to defend myself. I kept walking and moving my arms around until the door opened and the lights brightened.

I assumed a defensive stance, wishing I had a weapon. "Who are you and what do you want?"

The bearded man standing in the doorway put his hands up, palms out. "Whoah, there, it's okay. I'm your doctor. I won't hurt you."

I wasn't going to relax yet. "What happened? What's going on?"

"What do you remember?"

I shifted my stance slightly. "We were attacked by laser fire on the planet's surface. I was shot with a stunner and woke up here."

He slowly put his arms down. "Your group was attacked by the Varekai. They are ruthless pirates. My soldiers rescued you. You are lucky to be alive."

I frowned. "Why would pirates attack us?"

"We haven't determined what their motivations were. We did not detect their approach as they used advanced cloaking technology. By the time we realized what had happened, it was too late to help you. We don't have a transporter here at Maztec, so we couldn't get there quickly."

"Maztec?"

"Yes. Voyager Division has two underground bases here on Althar 3. Station Jannali is our main base of operations and Maztec is relatively new. My name is Dr Starrick and I'm in charge here. You're in safe hands."

I let my arms fall to my sides. I recalled something about a second base in our training, but hadn't paid much attention as we weren't going to be working there. I simply nodded.

His eyebrows rose. "Won't you sit down? You must be feeling terrible. I'll arrange some painkillers for your ailments."

I sat on the edge of the bed, looking down at my unfamiliar clothing and wishing I had some shoes. "Where are my clothes?"

He smiled. "They were filthy from the jungle, so we took the liberty of washing them for you. We don't have any clothing at the base large enough to fit a Shakiran, but I'm sure you'll find the clothes you're wearing comfortable enough. For that same reason, you'll have to wait for your own shoes to be cleaned and returned to you."

The white two-piece day suit I wore was uncomfortable and was a little too short in the sleeves and pant legs. What was even more uncomfortable was the unsettling thought of a stranger dressing me. "Who dressed me?" *And washed me...*

He smiled again but it didn't quite reach his eyes. "Don't worry. It was one of my female nurses."

That didn't make me feel much better. Some stranger had still seen me naked. Seen the scars on my body from years of combat training when I was too young to defend myself properly.

I ran my hands through my dishevelled hair. Why was he so casually talking about clothing when there were more pressing concerns here?

"Where are the others? Did anyone get hurt? I heard people screaming and saw someone running through the trees before we were found and stunned."

He shifted his weight and took a deep breath. "I am sorry to be the one to tell you this, but you are the only survivor."

CHAPTER 5

Never Too Early to Learn Life's Lessons

My stomach dropped. "What?" My voice was barely more than a whisper.

"The Varekai killed everyone and left you for dead. The ship was not damaged beyond a few scorch marks on the hull. Nothing of significance was taken. My men scared them off when they finally made it to the site."

He kept speaking, but I no longer heard his words. I was having trouble breathing. The faces of all the members of the crew filled my mind.

"No. It can't be right."

Zhenna. Mosuti. Bazeelia. Lanu. Kami...*Janssen*.

No no no no no!

I couldn't breathe.

I didn't even know the pilot's name, but he was gone too.

Tears filled my eyes. *This can't be happening.*

Dr Starrick rubbed his beard. "I'm afraid it is, my dear."

"But... I was just talking to Zhenna and Mosuti."

Why did everyone around me always die? I'd lost everyone in my family one by one. There was no one left. This job in the middle of nowhere was supposed to help me escape thoughts of death and a house full of memories for a while.

I couldn't make sense of it. Why was I the only survivor? Why would they stun me, but kill every other person? Zhenna and Mosuti were right there next to me in the leaf litter. Surely they'd used a stunner on them too? Unless the stunner was too powerful...

I stood and started pacing to try to combat the nervous energy raging inside me. "Why did they do it? What did they want? We didn't have anything valuable aboard the shuttle."

He scratched his ear. "We are still investigating the incident and the details are sketchy."

My heart pounded. I wanted to scream. Shout. Run.

Why?

I thought I'd toughened up. Thought I'd hardened my heart against this kind of pain. It had taken years to build up walls to protect my heart and in two short weeks, they'd been torn down completely.

I'd pushed Janssen away when I felt myself getting too close, and now he was gone. They were all gone. Tears stung my eyes again. My breathing was too shallow.

How had this happened? I had no answers.

My heart was shattered. The pieces scattered inside me. This was too much. I had suffered too much loss in my life. I was done.

"Larissa?"

I looked down at the doctor. I got the impression it wasn't the first time he'd called my name. "What?"

"We will get you fed and conduct some tests to see if you're undamaged after your ordeal, okay?"

I nodded, the word *undamaged* making me think of what that guy had said before I was shot.

I sat back down and stared at nothing. I knew the doctor was still talking, but I no longer cared.

Food was brought in and I was left alone to eat it. I didn't feel like eating, but I had no idea when I'd last had a meal. I didn't even know what time or even what day it was. So I sat and slowly ate a bowl of soup while I replayed conversations I'd had with all the crew members over and over in my head.

Then my mind took me back to when I was seven. The first blow in a long line of kicks life had given me. My brother, Eli, and I had been staying with my grandparents in the country to keep us safe from the bomb raids in the city during the war with the Zandarans. Our parents were in the military and had stayed in the city to do their duty.

Gran and Grandfather were already at the front door when I got there. They were looking out towards the car in the driveway with their mouths open.

Then Gran said, "Oh."

But it was the way she said it that struck me in the chest. Like all the air had drained from her lungs.

I looked up and she was shaking. Grandfather was grinding his teeth.

The man walking up to our door was not Father. Mother was not with him. He carried two neatly folded bundles of cloth with something shiny on top of each.

Where was Mother and Father? I thought they'd bought a new car and were here to take me and Eli home. I'd even started thinking about what to pack.

The man's feet made a loud, hollow sound as they clomped up the wooden front steps, then he stopped. "Are you Sameil and Jenaya Okada?"

"Yes," they both said. Their voices were shaky. Why were they shaky?

He held the bundles up in front of his chest. "I regret to inform you that your daughter, Orelia Malinya, and her husband, Ragnar Malinya, were killed during an air attack on our capital yesterday."

Gran's legs went a bit wobbly, but she didn't fall down. Grandfather didn't move.

Eli's voice came from behind me. "What are you talking about?"

The man bent forward a bit. "Apologies, young man. Were they your parents?"

"Yes."

"Your mother and father are not coming home. The place they work at was bombed."

No.

There was no air in the room.

Eli's face was red. He turned and ran to his room, slamming the door.

I couldn't move.

The man was talking to my grandparents again, but I couldn't hear properly. They sounded far away.

But they were going to take us back home. We were going to be a family again. Father was going to take us to see the ocean. We were going to see the sun set over the water. Mother was going to put her arms out to me and cuddle me and make me feel better, like these last few months were all a dream, like the war never happened.

Only, they weren't coming. Not now. Not ever.

The man was leaving. Gran held the bundles to her chest.

What were we going to do now? What would happen to Eli and I?

I opened my mouth to ask and nothing came out. There was nothing. I felt nothing.

At some point, someone shut the door. I still hadn't moved.

It wasn't fair.

They were going to come and get us. They promised. Father had gotten down on his knees and promised us a trip to the ocean. Mother had sat me on her lap and given me her necklace to look after until they came back.

A horrible feeling bubbled up in my chest. "But they promised! They said they'd come get us," I wailed.

Gran was there to pick me up, but I was so angry.

"It's okay, Larissa."

"No! It's not! They promised!"

Grandfather yelled out from the kitchen. "Don't coddle the child, Jenaya. She needs to learn the reality of war."

Gran held me tighter. "She is only seven."

"Never too early to learn life's lessons."

Then the back door slammed.

She carried me into the room I shared with Eli and we sat together in a huddle and cried.

I could still see Father clearly in my mind on my fifth birthday. He gave me a practice pistol and promised he'd teach me how to use it. I didn't think he would because he was always so busy with work, but he stayed with me all day until I could hit the targets with its soft bullets — most of the time. Work called and he told them he was busy training a new recruit. He promised he'd always be there for me when I needed him.

He promised.

I cried harder.

Now work had taken him away for good. He never would have been in the city if he wasn't a soldier. Mother wouldn't have been with him if she wasn't a soldier. They would have been here with us where it's safer. The ships only bombed the cities. They didn't worry about us out here in the hills.

The pain in my heart was so big, I thought I might die.

CHAPTER 6
I Think They Make You Look Quite Alluring

The pain was still there, even now.

If it wasn't for the war with the Zandarans, my parents would still be alive. Fighting was what we were taught to do, what we were *proud* to do, but that was wrong.

If there had been no war, we would have stayed in the city. Mother and Father would still be alive. We'd still be a family. There would be no broken promises.

And they wanted Eli and I to train to fight and join the war when we were old enough. I'd decided right then and there that I was not going to do it. I would not fight. I wouldn't cause someone else's family the unbearable pain I was feeling.

I pushed my soup aside, curled up on the bed and cried.

After breakfast the next day, the tests started. No one had come back into my room after I'd eaten the day before. I'd had a fitful sleep during the night, filled with dreams of laser fire and screams in the jungle.

My muscles felt like I'd been in combat training for twenty hours straight, a side-effect of being stunned. My eyes were gritty and my mouth had lost all moisture.

I didn't want to be poked and prodded. I wanted to block out the world. Grief threatened to drag me under and I wanted to let it.

A nurse fussed over the Bio-scan and I ignored her. I'd barely eaten my breakfast and refused to speak.

My mind replayed every interaction I'd had with Zhenna, Mosuti, Bazeelia, and Janssen, including the events in the jungle. On a loop.

I could almost feel Janssen's lips against mine.

I choked back a sob. My heart couldn't cope with the loss of more people I cared about. I was seven when I lost my parents. Fourteen when I'd lost my grandfather. Fifteen when Eli was killed. And now, at age twenty-one, Gran had died and left me alone. Besides Eli, it had been every seven years. Why did this keep happening to me?

I had no answers.

Gran had a heart attack while tending the garden she loved so much, but there was no one around to help her. I'd been away at university and couldn't stop the guilt from eating away at my soul. The doctor had told me there was nothing I could've done if I was there, that CPR wouldn't have helped, but it didn't make me feel any better.

I'd promised myself when I'd applied for this job that it would be a distraction and I could focus all my energy on my work. That way I would be able to build up a protective wall around my heart and somehow learn to cope with life on my own. My resolve quickly melted away when I'd met my new colleagues and realized I needed human company to stop me from losing my sanity.

My new resolve had been to make friends, but not get too close. To keep my distance.

And up until I'd lost them, I thought I'd succeeded.

Some of the tests didn't require much input from me, so I sat and endured them, but when they wanted me to run on a treadmill, I refused. The medical staff weren't happy, but I couldn't bring myself to care.

I just wanted to go home. This had all been a huge mistake.

I should have sold the house and started fresh, continued Gran's work of developing plants for medicinal purposes to heal the sick and save lives. Studying plants from other planets to help with my research was a stupid idea, especially now that it had all gone wrong.

I needed to go home.

The testing finally stopped and I was offered some lunch. I tried to eat, but my stomach was in knots.

Just as I'd given up on being able to force any more food into my mouth, Dr Starrick strode into the room with his fake smile in place. "How are we today?"

I looked away. My heart was still in pieces. My mind in turmoil.

He cleared his throat. "Miss Malinya, we have given you time to grieve your friends."

What — a few hours?

"You must understand that we need to make sure you are in good health as these pirates use unrated stunners that can sometimes do irreparable damage to the muscle tissue. We need to finish these tests."

Whatever. I was past caring about what damage might have been done to my muscles.

I continued to stare at the floor as he kept talking, but I wasn't listening.

I remembered the first time I'd had a conversation with Janssen aboard the Acronis. I was in the hydroponics bay checking out the exotic plants from Earth when he'd wandered in.

Movement caught my eye and I spun around, taking a defensive stance, but it was only Janssen.

He'd brought his arms up into position too, but he quickly turned his hands around, palms out. "Hey, it's just me," he said.

I relaxed. "Apologies. Habit."

He chuckled. "Yeah. Me too."

It was so ingrained in our lives that it was our first reaction — even after I'd refused to continue my combat training and had turned to botany.

We clasped each other's wrists, as is the custom on Shakira, and he smiled. "Janssen Malakua."

I returned the smile. "Larissa Malinya."

He raised an eyebrow. "So, it didn't take you long to seek out this place."

I looked up into his dark eyes. "Didn't take you long either."

We laughed.

I looked around the room. "As soon as I saw it on our tour, I knew I'd have to check it out and see the plants from Earth."

I showed him the sections I'd been looking at and we went through each bay, reading the cards and commenting on every type of plant. We were like children in a toy store, so excited over our discoveries. It seemed so natural to be sharing the experience with him. It would make working for Voyager Division more fun.

But I wasn't here to have fun... I pushed that thought away as we continued.

Once we'd reached the end of the last bay, Janssen looked into my eyes. "I couldn't help noticing that your eyes appear green in the light from the bays. It's not really noticeable most of the time."

My smile faded. "Yes. My grandmother on my mother's side was from Taon. Green is a common colour there."

I cringed inwardly, waiting for his reaction. It was usually a snide comment or look of disgust from other Shakirans.

His grin morphed into a full smile. "I think they make you look quite alluring."

My cheeks flushed as something fluttered in my chest. What could I say to that?

A tear rolled down my cheek at the memory.

"Miss Malinya!"

"What?"

There was a tight band around my chest making it hard to breathe.

How long had he been calling my name?

CHAPTER 7

It Was Finally Happening. I Was Losing It

"I will not tolerate this behaviour. You *will* cooperate with my medical team or I will *not* authorize your release to Station Jannali."

That got my attention.

Breathing became even harder. "I want to resign. I want to go home."

"You haven't even officially started working for Jannali and you want to resign?"

"Everyone on that ship was *killed*."

"That is no excuse for such a poor work ethic."

A poor work ethic? "You can't be serious."

He continued as if I hadn't spoken. "I'm not authorized to accept your resignation. You will have to wait until you get to Jannali and speak to Doctor Zoran Aimery about it. He is your superior within the company. And I am not going to let you go until I am satisfied that you are undamaged. You are overreacting to the loss of people you have known for only two short weeks and I am not satisfied that you are unaffected by the attack."

There was that word again. Undamaged. Why didn't he use the words *unhurt* or *uninjured*? It was like I was some kind of item of stock or machinery.

I sighed. If I wanted out, I had to do as I was told. "Okay. What do you want me to do?"

He squared his shoulders. "Follow me. We need to scan your brain."

⸻ ◆ ⸻

Being hooked up to an electroencephalograph to have my brain scanned was only the beginning. Over the next few days, they conducted many tests, but never once told me if my muscles and my brain were okay, no matter how many times I asked. It was beyond frustrating.

Surely I was well enough to leave. Or at the very least, they could continue their testing at Jannali.

I tried not to think about everything, but the grief was overwhelming. I made an effort to cooperate with the medical staff, but not because I was feeling any better. I was focused solely on transferring to Jannali and getting off this planet.

Images of the friends and family I'd lost kept flashing through my mind. I didn't know how I'd gotten through each day. Sleep was my only relief — but only if I didn't have any dreams.

On the seventh or eighth day, they hooked me up to the EEG for an extended amount of time and told me to lie still and relax. I almost lost my temper; I'd had enough rest and relaxation to last the rest of my life, and *way* too much time to think. It wasn't good for me. I couldn't turn my brain off. Sitting still was becoming increasingly hard.

I'd been exercising and running through some combat moves in the privacy of my room each day in order to keep myself fit. And sane. I never thought I'd be so keen to do those moves, but

38

with my present schedule of doing practically nothing, I needed it.

As the nurse took the wiring harness from my head, Dr Starrick strode in, head held high and fake smile in place. "How did you go?"

I frowned. "With what? These tests are the same as usual and I'm fed up with it all. Surely I can go to Jannali now, yes?"

The smile faded. "We've been over this. We have been testing for any long-term effects and the results are beginning to look good."

"*Beginning?* It's been more than a week, Doctor. I'm sure I would have shown some signs of nerve damage well before now. And surely they can continue these tests at Jannali in their own Medical Facility. I'm supposed to be working for the company as a botanist, not sitting here on my backside doing nothing."

"Please remain calm, Miss Malinya. We are doing the best we can. The electrical surge from the stunner was quite high and was probably the reason for the deaths of some of the others."

My mouth dropped open. This was the first time he'd mentioned anything about how or why the others had died.

"Why didn't you tell me about this before?"

"It took us a while to piece together the evidence from your tests and theirs. Their autopsies. We are now sure that its power was higher than that of a standard stunner."

I was confused. "But they go right up to a 'kill' setting, yes?"

He blinked several times. "Yes, of course. But this was a matter of the amps and ohms settings. You may not understand all of the elements involved. It's quite complicated."

I didn't fully grasp how the things worked, but I wasn't stupid, and what he said didn't make sense.

I wish she'd stop asking so many damned questions.

"Pardon?"

His eyebrows drew together. "I said that it is quite complicated."

"No. After that."

"I didn't say anything after that."

"But..."

I was sure he'd spoken.

His eyes seemed to light up. "How are you feeling now?"

I frowned. "Fine. Why?"

"I'm just checking to see how you are. Your health is important to us."

"Okaaay."

He was acting strange. I opened my mouth to ask more about the stunner, but closed it again. I wasn't sure how I could phrase my questions to get more information. He was such a frustrating man.

He cleared his throat and there was an intensity in his gaze. "You are free to go and have your lunch now. Nurse? Escort her back to her room."

My room? More like my prison cell.

I wanted to say something about being locked in, but I knew it was useless. I'd complained many times before and had gotten nowhere. I was biding my time, trying to do everything they asked of me so I could get out of here, but my patience was wearing thinner each day.

As I stood to leave, I thought I heard Starrick say something, but his mouth didn't move, so I dismissed it.

I followed the nurse out the door and down the hallway.

I'm so hungry. I need more than a salad today.

I frowned at the nurse, who usually didn't say a word to me unless it was absolutely necessary. "Apologies, what did you say?"

She looked up at me as if startled. "Nothing."

We kept walking and I wondered what was going on. I was positive she'd spoken to me. Or at least spoken to herself. Maybe she hadn't meant to say it out loud and was now embarrassed that I'd heard her. I tried to think about something else.

As we rounded a corner, there were three men standing together and they moved to the side to let us pass.

There's that insanely-tall Shakiran.

I turned toward them, but couldn't make out who'd said it.

Shit, can she hear me?

I stopped. "Who said that?"

They frowned.

"No one spoke," one of them said.

"I heard you."

She can *hear me. Damn. Think of nothing. Think of nothing.*

None of their mouths moved. The voice sounded like it was inside my head somehow. My heartbeat picked up.

Suddenly, I didn't feel well. I turned to the nurse. "I need to lie down."

She didn't say anything, just started walking, so I followed.

Think of nothing. Think of nothing...

What was going on here? Was I that distressed that I was starting to lose my sanity? My breathing became shallow. I had to try to remain calm.

I went straight to the bed and lay down once we'd reached my room.

The nurse stood at my bedside. "Are you okay? Do you need anything?"

Was I okay? No. Not at all. "No. I'm fine. I just need some time alone."

She simply nodded and left.

After the door slid shut, I could hear her voice in my head, muttering about what to have for lunch.

I closed my eyes. It was finally happening. I was losing it. Hearing voices. Imagining what people were saying.

CHAPTER 8

That Must Be Crazy Weird

Then something clicked in my mind. Was I imagining it? Or...
No.

No one in my family ever showed signs of being Talented. I
hadn't even met anyone with Talent till I'd met Mosuti.

It couldn't be right. How many Shakirans were Talented?
The rate was much lower than with other races... But what
about the Taonese? Gran was from Taon and the percentage of
people born with Talent was significantly higher. I took after
her with the green in my eyes and my height — I was shorter
than the average Shakiran.

It was a possibility, but was I only grasping at that answer
because the alternative was that I was losing my grip on reality?

It's happening. She's starting to read minds...

That was a male's voice.

I need to find out if he's in the lunch room...

That was a different person...

The voices kept coming and I couldn't keep up.

He said he'd call me at lunch time. Why hasn't he called?

I think I need a haircut...

These boots are hurting my feet...

I will need to check first to see if she's eating her lunch.

I covered my face with my hands. It was becoming too much.

The door slid open and a different nurse stepped in. "How are we going? Finished your... Haven't you ordered yourself some lunch yet?"

I looked up. Did she say that out loud? "Pardon?"

She was frowning. "Have you had your lunch yet?"

"No."

"Are you feeling okay? You look pale." *Well, paler than usual.*

Her mouth didn't move for that last sentence.

I hope she's not sick. I'm not trained to deal with Shakiran anatomy.

I needed to know if I was losing it. "Did you just think about not being trained to deal with Shakiran anatomy? Or am I going crazy?"

She blinked a few times and her face reddened. "I... Yes. You did read my mind. Sorry. I've never been that good with my mind shield."

I sat with my mouth hanging open. I was relieved that I wasn't losing it, but this was a surprising development. It had come from out of nowhere.

"They said you could be a Talent," she continued, "but I wasn't sure you'd be able to do telepathy after being here all this time without showing it."

"I haven't done this before now. I've never had any Talent. It just started happening."

Why would they have told her that I could be a Talent when the odds were stacked against it? Nothing was adding up here.

I could still hear the occasional words in my head, but I was trying to block them out so I could hear what she was saying.

"Oh. That must be crazy weird." She pulled out a Personal Com. "I better tell the doc then. It could be important."

Yes. I would have put it in my list of things that were important.

Why had this suddenly happened now? It was beyond just being unusual. Did a traumatic event cause Talent to be released or something? I'd never actually learned much about it. It had never been important. Shakira's enemies had never posed a threat in that area.

I'm late. Damn it. She'll be angry...

I wished I could block the voices out somehow. How did Mosuti cope?

"Doctor? Yes. I'm with Miss Malinya now. She said that she is experiencing a manifestation of Talent. Yes. She has been able to read some of my thoughts. Yes... No... She has never been able to before. Yes. Okay. Yes. Thank you. Bye."

He's so cute. How can I get him to notice me?

She put the Com back in her pocket. "He said he would like to run some tests on you."

"Of course he would."

I need to get ready for that procedure. It will be difficult, but...

"And you will need to be trained."

"What for?"

"To use your Talent. You can't just go around reading people's minds like this. It's not done. And it's not ethical. Or legal."

I supposed it wasn't. I wouldn't want someone to read my mind without my consent. Mosuti had asked for my permission and I'd given it gladly. The Talents' Code of Conduct was there to prevent this... but it wasn't like I was deliberately delving into their minds. It was like their thoughts were being thrown at me.

And it was another thing that would probably stop me from going to Jannali. I could bet credits on it.

I tried to push those thoughts aside and think of the benefits of my situation. Maybe being able to read minds could help me somehow in my goal to help save lives with my research. I needed to be trained properly if I wanted to make it a viable tool.

"I can start training here, then transfer to Jannali when I'm cleared by Doctor Starrick, yes?"

"I'm not sure how it works, but you will need to start training as soon as we can get things organized."

The voices were starting to get to me. "Can you ask him how to stop hearing everyone? It's starting to get a little overwhelming."

"What do you mean?"

"I can hear people talking in my head and it's very unsettling. I need to block them out somehow."

Her eyes widened. *I hope she can't hear everything I'm thinking.* "Oh, I'll call him back. I don't know anything about how to do that."

She called him up and told him what I'd said.

Once she'd ended the call, she told me they would organize someone to teach me how to block out people's thoughts.

"When?"

"They are seeing to it right now, so it should be soon."

"Okay. Thanks..." *I guess...*

While we waited for a call to say when someone could come, the voices kept coming, and some of them were personal thoughts. "Can't you tell these people to put up a mental shield or something? You teach that here, yes?"

"They try to get everyone to learn, but some are not good at it. And when there aren't any Talents around, we don't worry about doing it."

I stood and started pacing. "Well, it would help me immensely if they could block their thoughts from me…"

The door swished open and a slim man with dark hair walked in. He was probably tall by his race's standards, but only came up to my shoulder. He looked up at me with his eyebrows drawn together. "Hello, Miss Malinya. I am Conleth Jarecki. I've been sent to train you."

CHAPTER 9
There's Nothing You Can Do About It

I tried to smile. "Hello, Conleth. Thank you for coming right away. I need help to block out everyone's voices."

He smiled. "Yes, I know. Have you tried strengthening your mental shield?"

I frowned. "I don't have one."

His eyes widened. "What? Why not? Everyone receives training on how to create a mental shield."

"Not on Shakira. We've never needed it."

He rolled his eyes. "Well, clearly you do."

I crossed my arms. "Talent is not common on Shakira. And it isn't my fault that my elders don't think it's important enough to include in my training. Then there's the fact that I've never been off-world before."

He sighed heavily. "Okay, so we'll simply have to start from scratch."

I didn't like this man, but I needed him if I wanted the voices to stop. "What do I need to do?"

He grabbed the chair and spun it around to face me, but gestured to the bed. "Sit on the side of the bed. Make yourself comfortable."

He waited till I'd sat down before he lowered himself onto the chair.

"Now, I need you to take a few deep breaths and relax." I did as he said. "Close your eyes." He spoke slowly, pausing between each sentence. "Now try to look inwards. Into your mind. Imagine you're standing on a flat stretch of ground. Now imagine building a wall in front of you, one brick at a time. Then build it around you. The wall is soundproof. The wall is getting higher. The voices are growing dim as the wall gets higher."

I could picture the wall and built it up the way he'd described.

"Okay, keep building. It's getting higher. It's arching over on all sides, meeting in the middle, and covering you completely. The voices can't get through. They are fading to nothing. Now they are gone."

The voices faded, but I couldn't get them to stop. "I can still hear them. It's not working."

"Don't give up."

The voices flooded in again and my eyes flew open. "I can't do it."

He didn't move. "That wasn't too bad for a first try. Go again. Start from the ground and build the wall again. Close your eyes. Go. You can do it."

I took a deep breath and tried again. And again. Each time I tried, it became easier to block them out, so I kept going.

Each time I failed, he simply said, "Again."

By the end of it, I felt drained, but he insisted that I keep holding the wall in place. "Once you get the hang of it, it will become second nature and won't take much effort to maintain."

I hoped he was right because the energy seemed to seep from my body like a bleeding wound.

The silence in my head was bliss. "Thank you. I thought I'd never be able to shut it off."

"You're welcome." He sucked in a long breath and blew it out slowly. "Now that we have that out of the way, we need to find out how much you know about Talent and teach you to block your thoughts from others."

"What do you mean?"

"Sometimes you accidentally broadcast your thoughts and other Talents can hear you without even trying to read your mind."

My stomach dropped.

What? "You can't be serious."

"Yes. I'm definitely serious. I've heard some of your thoughts — but don't worry — they weren't really personal. Just you telling yourself to concentrate and whatnot."

My heart beat faster. People could hear what I was actually thinking?

My mind scrambled to remember what I'd been thinking about since all this started. I didn't think it had been anything embarrassing, but I wasn't sure. My face heated.

I would have to be extremely careful what I thought about until I could get this under control.

Shame flowed through me — Shakirans were highly disciplined and always in control — but I pushed those thoughts aside. This attitude had been instilled in us from an early age, but I was determined to resist it. I was *not* a warrior. And this was new. Totally different to anything I'd ever experienced. Of course I wouldn't be in control.

I took a deep breath and reigned in my thoughts.

I looked Conleth in the eye. "Please, tell me how to block my thoughts."

"All in good time. I need to explain some things about—"

"No. This is embarrassing. Tell me now. I need to make sure no one can hear me."

He sighed. "Alright."

I was sure he'd rather be anywhere else, but I had to get this right.

He leaned forward. "Okay. This one is the normal mental shield that everyone is taught to create. It's usually used to protect you from telepathic intrusion, so it's important for everyone to master."

I nodded. *Just hurry up and teach me...*

"Okay, so the wall you built in your mind can also be used to block your thoughts from others. You need to concentrate on it and will it to hold in your private thoughts and block any outside attempts to read your mind. It's kind of hard to explain, but relatively easy to do. Do you understand?"

"Yes, I think so."

"Okay. Close your eyes and try it now."

It wasn't as simple as I thought it would be, but once I'd worked out how to keep my thoughts inside the wall, it became easy. It wasn't much different to what I'd already done.

I practiced keeping the wall in place while Conleth tried to read my mind, with fairly good results.

I sighed. It would take a bit of getting used to, but maybe I could do this.

Conleth cleared his throat. "Now. Have you heard of the Talents' Code of Conduct?"

"Yes. Of course I have."

"You will need to be very familiar with it now that you have manifested some Talent. I will give you a copy on a small screen for you to read and memorize."

"Okay."

My mind tried again to find ways for me to use telepathy to somehow aid me in finding medicinal uses for my plants. I couldn't see a connection, but I wouldn't give up. Surely I could make it work somehow.

⸻ ◆ ⸻

In between all the tests over the next three days, Conleth taught me how to hold a telepathic conversation by sending my thoughts to his mind. It wasn't too different from what Mosuti had shown me. Instead of only thinking the thought in the forefront of my mind, I needed to seek out the other person's mind and push the thought to them.

It was a balancing act between speaking telepathically and keeping my mental shield in place the whole time, but I was getting the hang of it.

Thinking of Mosuti and the other friends I'd lost was difficult, but I had to push through it. I had to try to force those emotions into a box and pack them away.

As we were finishing up our lesson for the day, a guy who looked too young to be working here knocked and entered with a message that Dr Starrick wanted me to go to Lab Four. I sighed. I didn't see the point in the continuous testing. I needed to get out of here and go home.

"Don't sigh," Conleth told me. *"Doctor Starrick is only doing what's best for you at this point."*

I looked at him. *"He's had almost two weeks to check me over and see if I'm okay. I should be allowed to go to Jannali now."*

It was his turn to sigh. *"We've been over this. And now that you've shown that you have a telepathic ability that you need to learn to control, things have taken longer to complete."*

I resisted the urge to roll my eyes. *"I have learnt to control it. Surely I can continue training at Jannali."*

"We need to be sure that you have enough *control so that you don't breach the Code. Have you read all of the Code of Conduct yet?"*

"Yes. Three times. There's nothing else to do when I'm not here with you or being poked at by scientists."

"Don't be disrespectful."

Now I had to resist the urge to grit my teeth and growl. I wasn't normally like this — it was not honourable behaviour — but my body itched to go, to get out of here. To run. I'd been here for eleven days with no answers and no hope of going to Jannali anytime soon.

Something was very wrong here.

Besides being locked in my room and having an escort wherever I went, I wasn't allowed any outside communication. There had to be more to this than what I was being told. It was beyond frustrating.

I had to bide my time till I could get out, then tell Dr Aimery what was happening here.

From what I'd been told, Maztec and Jannali were underground bases with nothing but dense jungle on the planet's surface above them, so trying to escape would be foolish — if it was even possible. We'd often gone camping when I was a child, but that wouldn't be enough to help me survive a rainforest full of prehistoric creatures and barbaric natives.

I quickly pushed images of the jungle from my mind.

Conleth stood. *"Let's go then. Doctor Starrick will be waiting."*

I dragged myself to my feet and followed him.

As soon as the door to Lab Four swished open, Dr Starrick looked up from his tablet on a desk full of medical equipment. "It's about time. Where have you been?"

I frowned. "We came straight here after receiving your message."

"Not good enough. I sent that boy to you over half an hour ago." He ran a hand over his beard. "Sit."

I sat in the chair he'd indicated and tried not to react. I'd learnt that questioning him led to a lecture on how he'd saved my life and was only looking out for my health and best interests and so on.

I'd had enough of being treated like a child.

I looked over my shoulder; Conleth was gone. I didn't blame him.

Starrick attached some wires to my hand. "Now, I am going to test your nerves in your right arm and hand, so you need to keep perfectly still for the first part, okay?"

I nodded and bit the inside of my cheek to keep from saying anything. He was well aware that I'd had this test done five times before.

He turned to the nurse sitting at the computer console. "Well?"

She grimaced. "The computer is still initializing, Doctor."

He swore under his breath and continued fussing with the wires.

I tried to relax, but he was so angry. He was always impatient and arrogant, but today, he was quite hostile.

After we'd gotten started, he turned to me. "I said to keep *still*, you silly girl!"

"I *was* keeping still."

"You moved your thumb. Now I will have to start again."

I pursed my lips. If I said what was on my mind, I would never get out of this place.

I took a deep breath. *You can do this. Just keep calm. Imagine sitting on the bench in the garden at home, the smell of the Delphinas...*

Only, thinking about that made me think of Gran. And Eli.

I'd begged Eli not to join the military, but he'd had his heart set on doing his part for Shakira and there was no stopping him.

I'd begged him. I'd screamed at him. But he'd left anyway. Family pride and a lifetime's worth of conditioning overruled a sister's love.

He'd only been flying missions for four months when his ship had been shot down over the planet Valora, killing him instantly.

My eyes stung with unshed tears and I forced myself to think of something else.

Starrick took the wires off me before moving on to my other hand and both my feet. Once he'd finished, I wasn't free to go. I was directed to move to the bed and the nurse put the wiring harness on my head carefully while Starrick told her she was doing it wrong at every turn.

Why didn't he do it himself? Why did he have to treat her like that? He was such an arrogant, pig-headed man with not a shred of integrity.

I stared at his knitted brow and his down-turned mouth. The poor girl was close to tears and I clenched my fists.

He yelled at her again, but I'd had enough. "Stop it! Stop treating her like this. It's a disgraceful misuse of your position."

They both stared at me and I glared at him. I felt a blow to the cheek and my head jerked to the side, knocking the wiring harness sideways. I would normally have blocked an attack like that, but it was so unexpected. I turned back to Starrick, my mouth hanging open.

"You will *not* speak to me like that. You will do as I say or you will never leave this place." His eyes narrowed. "In case it has escaped your notice, we are on a small primitive planet at the edge of the Known Universe. I will treat my staff and my patients any way I please and there's nothing you can do about it."

CHAPTER 10
Your Training Starts Now

I clamped my mouth shut. I couldn't say any of the words racing through my mind; I would never get out of here.

He looked more closely at the wiring harness and swore. "Now look what you've done. The harness is broken. Nurse, get her out of my sight."

What *I'd* done? Seriously?

My anger rose despite his warning and the pain in my cheek. I clenched my jaw and glared at him while he mumbled under his breath and the nurse removed the harness from my head.

Something shattered behind me and I turned to find scattered pieces of glass on the floor.

Starrick glared at the nurse. "What happened?"

She cringed. "I don't kno—"

"Why are you so careless with the equipment?"

"I'm not. I put it up against the wall, nowhere near the edge. I don't understand how it could have fallen."

"You *must* have put it near the edge. Things don't fall to the floor on their own."

I couldn't help frowning. If she was telling the truth, then what had happened? Was she telekinetic?

As far as I knew, she wasn't, and neither was the doctor...

The nurse gave me a little sideways glance and quickly looked away.

That left *me…*

No.

That couldn't be possible. There had to be some other explanation. I tried to push the idea from my mind, but it wouldn't budge.

The nurse was ordered to clean up the mess and once she'd finished, she ushered me out of the room. I was glad to be finally out of there.

⸺◦⸺

I'd been thinking about that shattered glass bottle all night and all morning. Could it have been me?

I'd heard that people with more than one ability usually developed other abilities soon after the first. It could be that I'd also developed a telekinetic ability.

So what did that mean? What did it mean for me? How would it change my life? The telepathy had already changed things, but being able to move objects with my mind was a whole new challenge.

Was there a way to use this Talent too? That is, if I *did* have it.

How would I know for sure? How could I test it? I had no idea.

As if on cue, there was a knock at the door and it swished open to admit Conleth. He was the only person who bothered to knock first, even if he did barge in straight after.

58

He gave me an odd smile, probably noticing the slight bruising under my left eye from the slap in the face. "How are we today?"

It was weird to me the way he used the term *we* rather than *you*, but I forced myself to ignore it. "I am bored, as usual. You?"

"Don't be sarcastic. Let's get started."

I sat on the edge of the bed. "That wasn't me being sarcastic. I am quite serious."

He sighed. *"Well then, maybe you should change your attitude. We are trying to help you here."*

"It doesn't look like it from where I'm standing. I want to go to Jannali and quit and go home."

"You should be practicing your telepathic skills. Stop speaking aloud."

I pushed some hair back over my shoulder and sighed heavily. They'd returned my beads and hair ties a couple of days after I'd woken up here, but I hadn't bothered putting them in my hair. For most of my life, I'd put thin braids in my hair that were interspersed with beads. Lately, I hadn't cared about what I looked like. Being locked up was getting to me. No amount of exercise, combat moves, or meditation was going to calm me. The restlessness seemed to come from inside my soul.

He sat down on the chair. *"Come on. You need to practice this."*

"I know!"

"Well, do it!"

"No!"

As I shouted, a cup flew off the table, bounced off the wall, and rolled onto the floor.

Conleth stared at the cup as if it was going to jump up and attack him, then looked at me. I could see him putting it together in his mind. "You're a Kinetic too?"

I looked back at the cup. "I... don't know. Do you think that was me?"

"Well, it certainly wasn't me."

I ran a hand through my hair. "What happens now?"

"I tell the doctor and we start your training immediately. Telekinesis can be dangerous if it's not under control."

I shifted my position on the bed. He pulled out his Personal Com and contacted Starrick, who didn't take long to arrive, excitement lighting his eyes.

He was eager to see what I could do.

I cringed inwardly. "I don't know how to show you. I don't even know if it was me."

He frowned and turned to Conleth. "I thought you said she could move objects with her mind."

Conleth ran a hand through his hair. "I did. She did it. She moved a cup. It fell on the floor."

Starrick looked up at me.

I shrugged. "Maybe it wasn't me. Maybe it was Conleth."

Conleth crossed his arms. "It definitely wasn't me. I'm not a Kinetic. And it didn't just fall over. It flew across the room. That had to be you. You were angry."

Like yesterday. Maybe it *was* me. *Both* times.

I had to accept the fact that I'd manifested another ability within days of the first.

"Okay. What do I have to do?"

Starrick crossed his arms too. "Your training starts now. Your new ability is more dangerous than the telepathy. People could be seriously hurt if you get upset and start hurling objects around the room."

I imagined the cup and other loose items in the room flying through the air and cringed. I nodded.

I didn't want to accidentally hurt myself or anyone else. I needed to get a handle on this one asap.

Starrick turned on his heel. "Get it done, Jarecki. Then report back to me."

Conleth took a deep breath and let it out slowly. "Okay, let's do this."

I turned to him. "What?"

He frowned. "You heard Doctor Starrick. You need to learn control immediately."

"Yes, but how are you going to teach me? You just said you're not a Kinetic."

He swallowed. "I'm not, but we don't have anyone available that has that ability. We will have to make do."

I crossed my arms. "What about at Jannali?" He went a little pale. "Maybe they could send someone over here if I'm not allowed to go there."

"No. They don't have anyone available at the moment. They're busy. They're the main base on this planet. They've been here longer than us. I will teach you."

I stared at him. There was always a reason why I couldn't do this or that, or why I couldn't go to Jannali. Why were they keeping me from going there?

And how was I supposed to learn from someone with zero experience in telekinesis?

"Don't look at me like that. It won't be that hard."

Yeah? That's what you think.

CHAPTER 11

I Thought You Were Dead!

He rubbed his hands together. "Let's get started."

I resisted the urge to sigh. "Okay. What do I have to do?"

"Let's start with the cup. You already moved it." He retrieved it and placed it on the table in front of me and cleared his throat. "Concentrate on the cup and imagine there is a force inside you trying to get free. Feel it build up and once it has gathered, push it toward the cup."

I nodded. I wasn't sure what he meant, but I tried to find something like what he was talking about.

"There's nothing. I can't find anything."

"Maybe it's not strong enough yet or something. Maybe you're not looking hard enough or in the right place."

I tried again.

Still nothing. Maybe it would work better with someone who knew what they were doing.

I looked at him.

He nodded. "Keep trying. You didn't think you would get it first try, did you? Remember how many tries it took before you built up your wall?"

I nodded.

But I'd had someone who knew what they were doing to guide me.

"So, keep at it. You'll get there."

I tried, but nothing happened. I didn't know what I was doing. "Surely there is someone else who knows how to do this."

"No. There's no one. Now do it."

I'm not sure how many times I tried, but eventually I gave up concentrating on the cup. I closed my eyes and looked inward. I slowed my breathing and relaxed.

Finally, I felt something there. A tiny spark of energy, but it was there.

I coaxed it out and it became bigger. I imagined it growing and pushed it down my arm and into my hand. Then I pushed it out toward the cup and opened my eyes to see it fly backwards into the wall again, making us both jump.

"Yes! You did it!"

He seemed as surprised as I was.

I took a deep breath; I felt drained. How much energy did this take?

Maybe it would take less energy when I'd gotten used to it, like the telepathy.

I could do this. I would find out how to use this to my advantage. Maybe even use it to get out of here... Somehow.

Conleth breathed in. "Right. Try again. We need you to be able to lift the cup up with some control now that you've worked out how to move it."

I sucked in a breath. *Let's do this.*

<hr>

The next morning, I had my breakfast and showered, ready for whatever they had planned for me, but was surprised when

Conleth didn't come in for a lesson. The nurses didn't come in to poke at me or take me to a lab. Starrick didn't show his face either. If the tests were no longer needed, I would have been happy, but no one had said anything about it the day before. This wasn't right.

I sat at my table and tried to relax and sit still, but started pacing instead.

As it approached lunch time I began to worry. There had to be something wrong. I wondered what could have happened to break them from their routine.

I started to hope that they hadn't come in because they were taking me to Jannali today, but that was foolish. I couldn't afford to hope.

I decided to do some stretches before someone came in, just to calm my mind. I started with jogging on the spot to warm up my muscles, then did some arm swings and stretches. As I moved on to my leg stretches, I heard someone scream, followed by what sounded like laser fire.

My heart leapt into my throat and scenes from the attack in the jungle flashed through my mind. What was happening out there?

As the sounds became louder, I put my shoes back on and looked around for something I could use to defend myself if anyone came in here. All I had was the table, so I turned it on its side and dragged it to the door. Standing behind it didn't make me feel any safer, but there was nothing else unless I dragged the bed over.

My hands gripped the edge of the table as more screaming and yelling and laser fire rent the air.

The adrenalin was rushing through me as I pushed the table closer to the door, ready to lift it up in front of me if someone entered.

My heart pounded and I couldn't slow my breathing.

As soon as the door swished open, I charged forward with the table in front of me. It wouldn't stop a laser blast, but I was hoping the element of surprise would help me.

As I pushed forward, I used some kinetic power to lift the table without even thinking about it.

I hit something and heard a grunt and before I knew it, the table and I were falling on top of someone. A pistol discharged as we fell back, firing back toward the door instead of at me. I looked up to see a man standing in the doorway with a blackened hole in his chest and a look of astonishment on his face. He collapsed to the floor and the smell of burnt flesh made me gag.

I quickly got to my feet ready to fight, looking around for possible threats. The man I'd landed on was unconscious. I stared at the other man's lifeless body, his eyes staring at nothing. I hadn't pulled the trigger, but I'd caused him to die. My face was cold.

I'd trained for this for half of my life, but to be looking at a dead body, knowing I caused their death, was something entirely different. His family would experience the pain I'd lived with since I was seven. This was exactly why I'd chosen not to pursue a career in the armed forces. I did *not* want to cause anyone the soul-crushing despair that comes with losing a loved-one.

Shouts from down the hallway jolted me into action. Someone could walk around the corner at any second. The guy under the table could come to. I had to run. I turned away from the sounds and tried not to make too much noise as my shoes slapped against the vinyl floor.

I'd never been in this section of the base before, so I had no idea where I was going. I wandered through the halls, avoiding the sound of laser fire every chance I got. Then it occurred to me that I should have armed myself when I had the chance. It was too late to go back and I couldn't find my way back anyway.

I turned a corner and almost ran into someone. My first reaction was to duck back around the corner to avoid being shot, but I caught a glimpse of his face as I stepped back and it was like seeing a ghost.

He looked up at me, wide-eyed. "Larissa! You're alive!"

"Mosuti? I thought you were dead!"

CHAPTER 12
Please, Let There Be More

I couldn't believe it. There was an ache in my chest and I had to fight the tears that were threatening to fall. He wrapped me in a tight hug, but we pulled away from each other when we heard footsteps heading our way.

He grabbed my hand. "This way. Hurry."

I let him lead me down a series of hallways and into a storage room full of old computer equipment, my brain still stuck on how it was even possible that he was alive.

He pointed under a desk in the corner and I heard his voice in my head. *"Under there."*

We crawled under and sat with our knees pulled up to our chests and I was thankful that we weren't visible from the doorway.

I sent a thought to his mind. *"Guess what?"*

His eyebrows rose and a smile split his face. *"When did this happen?"*

I returned his smile. *"About five days ago. It came out of nowhere."*

"It usually does. It's freaky." Then he frowned. *"It is uncommon on Shakira, yes?"*

"Yes. That's what took me by surprise. I don't know anyone with Talent. Except you."

We sat in silence for a while.

I fidgeted with my shoe. *"Then yesterday I found out I'm also a Kinetic."*

"Really? Wow. That's great. I'm a Telepath and Empath; you already knew about the telepathy. Have you been Rated yet?"

"Rated?"

"Yes. You'll need to be tested to see which abilities you have and how strong they are. It's very useful for deciding your possible career path. You'll be given a Rating from one to ten, one being the strongest. I am a T2 in telepathy and T4 in empathy."

I tried to process that, but there were more pressing things to worry about. *"Do you know what's going on?"*

"Not a clue. I've been here since the attack in the jungle — locked in my room — and they told me I was the only survivor."

My chest tightened. *"That's what they told me. Then they said they had to run tests to see if there was any nerve damage from the illegal stunners the Varekai used."*

"Yeah, same. They've obviously lied about who survived, so what else have they lied about?"

A spark of hope ignited in my chest. *"What if everyone survived and Starrick has been keeping us apart the whole time?"*

"It's possible, I guess..."

I had to squash that thought in case I was wrong. I couldn't afford to hope, only to find they were actually gone. I knew I shouldn't have let these people into my heart and now the pain was crushing me all over again. I tried to fight it. I fought back tears and tried to shove those emotions down deep. I had to stay strong and keep it together. We weren't out of this yet. I couldn't fall apart right now.

I pushed all those emotions away. Buried them deeper.

We sat for a long while in silence, listening for any sounds that might give a clue as to what was happening out there.

At the sudden sound of the door opening, I jumped, then held my breath, hoping we wouldn't be discovered.

A man came around the stack of boxes in the middle of the room and pointed a laser pistol at us. "Identify yourselves!"

We raised our hands and my heart was in my throat. "Larissa Malinya!"

"Mosuti Kyah!"

He lowered his weapon. "You're the people we've been looking for. It's okay. We're here to help. We're from Station Jannali, sent to get you guys out of here."

Hope bloomed in my chest. We were finally getting out of this hellish place.

"Are you injured?"

We both shook our heads.

The man spoke into his Com. "We've found two more. Uninjured. Yes. I'll bring them in right away." He turned to us. "I'm Private Rowton. Please come with me."

We scrambled to our feet and Mosuti started to ask questions. "What's going on? Who's doing all the shooting?"

Rowton looked over his shoulder. "Soldiers loyal to Doctor Starrick were given the order to terminate all the people they've been holding here and running experiments on. You're lucky to have escaped your rooms when you did."

A chill ran down my spine. Those men would have shot me and simply moved on to the next room if I hadn't defended myself. I still felt terrible about the man's death, but it was either him or me.

As we walked through the now-quiet halls, my mind reeled. Starrick had been running experiments on us? What kind of experiments, and why? And he'd ordered those men to kill us. Was that an attempt to cover everything up? What made him think shooting us would work? There was no time to dispose of the evidence before the people from Jannali came in...

We wouldn't have been able to talk and tell them what had happened to us...

Soon we came to a large area full of people. I searched their faces, hoping to find someone familiar, and as Zhenna turned our way, my heart leapt.

Another friend I thought I'd lost was alive.

I rushed forward and wrapped my arms around her and was soon joined by Mosuti. "It's so good to see you."

She pulled away a bit and looked up into our faces and whispered, "I thought you were both dead."

"We thought *you* were," Mosuti said. "Looks like they told us all the same story."

Zhenna looked at him. "There are others?"

"I don't know. I certainly hope so."

I cursed myself for the feelings of hope tearing at my chest. *Please, let there be more. Let Janssen be here.*

We searched, but there were no familiar faces in the crowd. My heart sank a little and I told myself not to hold out hope for anyone else. It seemed I would probably have to accept the fact that Janssen and the others were gone.

We were teleported in groups of three across to Jannali by one of the Talents, then taken to the Medical Facility. Being teleported made me feel dizzy, but I was told it was normal. While the nurses checked us over, I tried to be as accurate as I could as I answered their questions.

After being cleared, we were told we would be briefed by the doctor in charge at Jannali and I couldn't help the sinking feeling in my stomach when I thought about what the doctor in charge of Maztec was like.

They ushered us into the briefing room and we sat at a large oval table waiting for Dr Aimery to arrive. Zhenna fidgeted with her necklace and Mosuti tapped a finger on his leg while I tried to sit perfectly still — and failed. I shifted in my seat and pushed my hair behind my ear, then crossed my legs. Grandfather would have been disappointed. A Shakiran should always be poised and disciplined. I needed to be better than this. What would Eli—

I stopped. What did it matter? Anyone in my family who would have chastised me was long gone...

Zhenna sighed. "This waiting is driving me crazy. I'm dying to know if anyone else survived."

Mosuti scratched his chin. "Maybe we're it. We didn't see any others in that group at Maztec or at the Medical Facility."

"They could be holding them separately."

"It seems unlikely. I guess we'll have to wait and see."

Zhenna started to pace and I resisted the urge to join her.

The door whooshed open and a heavy-set man with a greying beard strode in, followed by a group of people; I recognised some of them from the rescue party as they sat down.

"Good afternoon," he began. "I am Doctor Zoran Aimery and I am in charge here at Station Jannali."

We said our greetings and waited for answers. Thoughts that he might be like Starrick crept into my mind again and I pushed them down. I had to give this man a chance. But if he was like Starrick, we were in deep trouble.

He cleared his throat. "I'm sorry for hitting you with so many questions and for keeping you waiting. No doubt you have questions of your own, but we've had a lot of data to sort through and we're still interviewing people from Maztec. A few days ago, we received a report that Doctor Starrick was conducting illegal experiments over at Maztec, so we sent a couple of undercover teams to investigate. But the moment their presence was discovered, things went a little haywire and Starrick's people opened fire.

"We didn't find Starrick, however. He is apparently out in the jungle looking for a person who had escaped from the base. His people contacted him once our teams were discovered and he gave the order to terminate all 'specimens' that they were conducting these experiments on. The two of you managed to escape from your rooms and Zhenna was fortunate enough to be found by our people, so you are the only survivors from the labs."

Pain stabbed at my chest and Zhenna sucked in a breath.

Janssen was really gone.

CHAPTER 13
That Was Me

Guilt that I'd only thought of Janssen slammed into me, but I couldn't help it. He was the one I'd spent the most time with. All those conversations in the hydroponics garden and... And I'd let him get too close to my heart.

I pushed those thoughts away.

I had to accept — all over again — that they were gone.

I didn't know the pilot at all. Kami was a painful person to be around, but didn't deserve to die. Lanu was a nice guy, full of enthusiasm. Bazeelia was fun and always bubbly and didn't make me feel freakishly tall whenever she was near.

Dr Aimery consulted his Palm-pad. "I'll try to give you the information that we have so far, but the investigation is ongoing. The men that attacked you at the Outrider's landing site were not pirates. They were, in fact, Doctor Starrick's men sent there to capture you. They did, however, kill the pilot immediately so he wouldn't recognise their uniforms."

I clenched my fists. They thought they could do whatever they liked out here on the Fringe. Dr Starrick even said it to my face.

"The scientist who gave the order for you to collect samples while the pilot made his repairs has now been arrested. That order did *not* come from me. This man was working with Starrick and had created the perfect opportunity for Starrick's men to capture you and make it look like an attack from the Varekai. It was all a setup."

I turned to Dr Aimery. "I remember thinking that it was irresponsible of the company to send us out into the jungle unarmed considering how dangerous the wildlife is."

"Yes. That's exactly why I would not have put you in danger like that."

I sighed heavily. It was hard to comprehend that we'd been set up.

Dr Aimery cleared his throat. "All of you were taken to Station Maztec and kept in separate rooms, and by the sounds of it, you were all told you were the only survivor."

We all nodded.

"Now, have any of you heard of the Eibhlin Process?"

Zhenna and Mosuti nodded, but I shook my head.

"Okay. It's a variation of the original process — called the Verum Process — have you heard of that one?" I shook my head again. "Well, when a person has brain damage from a head injury, the doctors wait until it heals physically. The Verum Process is then used to detect and map the damaged areas of a patient's brain using a modified electroencephalograph. The next step is to map the same areas of a healthy brain. The mapped areas of the healthy brain are transferred to the damaged brain, thereby replacing those messed up thought processes. It is quite a successful procedure when used properly."

He paused to let that sink in. I cringed. How many times had I been hooked up to an EEG while I was at Maztec?

"The Eibhlin Process, however, transfers the entire mapped brain to another's mind, wiping out the consciousness and memories and replacing them completely. This is almost like murder because the second person's mind is wiped from existence."

That would be like a body swap. You'd wake up in another body. A shiver ran down my spine.

"Also, it doesn't affect the first person at all, so you will find that there would be two people with the same mind. It can be quite disturbing.

"People have used this procedure to escape an ageing body or one with failing health. It's illegal throughout the Known Universe. Doctor Starrick was involved in developing this process and was suspected of continuing to practice it after it was outlawed. And now we have proof that he is not only practicing it, but running experiments to improve the process."

So this is the type of experimentation he'd been playing with? I shuddered. What had he done to me while those wires were on my head?

Dr Aimery took a deep breath and let it out slowly. "We're still sorting through the data and I want to try to address each situation separately. So firstly, Lanu Ricksha and Kami Olion were among those that were killed after some of the experiments went awry."

I tried to keep my breathing steady, dreading his next words.

He looked directly at me and I sucked in a breath. "Larissa's consciousness was transferred to Bazeelia Shamari's mind and it didn't map correctly. She went a little crazy and trashed her room and assaulted staff, so she was killed."

I sucked in a breath.

Poor Bazeelia.

Wait — she wasn't Bazeelia anymore when they killed her. That was *me*.

My chest tightened as I tried to imagine it.

"Mosuti's mind was transferred to a man named Kaylan Bartoff. He was a cleaner working on the base. His was another failure and he could barely even talk. He was killed after our raid started, along with some of the natives of this planet that Starrick had captured without our knowledge or the company's approval."

I studied Mosuti's face as he absorbed this. He was definitely horrified by this news. My face probably looked the same.

"Before we get to Zhenna, I need to inform you that there are no records at the base so far that mention Janssen Malakua. We suspect that he was able to avoid capture and is still out there in the jungle — if he has managed to survive the dangerous conditions."

My heart stuttered. Could I dare to hope that he was still alive?

NO! My mind screamed. *Don't hope. Don't you dare hope.*

Dr Aimery placed his Palm-pad down on the table carefully. "Okay, so Zhenna's consciousness was successfully transferred to that of a native woman. This native is from a race of people called the Waikari who have evolved to live above and below the ocean. They have gills and lungs. They are also telepathic. The telepathy has probably evolved to allow them to communicate underwater."

Zhenna took a deep breath and ran her fingers through her hair.

Wow. I tried to imagine swimming underwater without any breathing apparatus. Then I remembered the first part of what he'd said. Zhenna's mind was in this woman's body, and Zhenna was also sitting next to me.

"Some of the Waikari have other abilities," he continued, "and we've been told that this woman is also a Kinetic and Empath. Her Talent is very strong."

This was getting more bizarre by the second.

I frowned. "I don't remember anything in our briefings about an amphibious race of people."

"No, you wouldn't have. Starrick discovered them recently and kept them a secret. He kept records on a separate computer network to our own."

Zhenna leaned forward. "So, how does this even work, Doctor? How can there be two of me? I'm trying to understand."

He turned to face her. "You're not alone, dear. It's difficult for all of us to get our heads around. The thing we need to remember is, she *is* Zhenna. She has all your memories and thought processes. She doesn't know you survived. She thinks she's you and technically, she is."

My mind struggled to comprehend that there were now two Zhenna Rhodarmas. It would be weird if they were in the same room together.

Dr Aimery ran a hand over his beard. "She is now in an alien body and has had to deal with that, and I assume that from the moment the procedure was complete and she began experiencing a different set of circumstances to you, she started to change. Her situation is drastically different from yours as we speak. We are all products of our upbringing and life experiences after all." He paused. "She has retained the Waikari woman's memories — which was the result of one of their experiments — and she reports that it's almost like there are two people in her head. It's all very confusing and she has tried to deal with it by changing her name. She has named herself Tamisan as she no longer feels like Zhenna or the Waikari woman..." He consulted his Palm-pad. "Sifayah, her name was. Zhenna — Tamisan — has gained Sifayah's Talent as well."

My mind reeled. This sounded so far-fetched, yet for some reason, I believed him.

Zhenna's cheeks were wet with tears and Mosuti looked shaken.

I leaned forward. "You've spoken to her?"

"Not personally. She made contact with one of our Telepaths, Darion Andiyar, through telepathy. Tamisan is the person I mentioned earlier who escaped from Maztec and is still out there in the jungle." My heart clenched. "She and Darion have kept in contact with one another and we've sent a team to find her and bring her here."

I imagined Zhenna trying to survive in that wild jungle. She was a city girl and didn't have even the most basic camping skills. "How in the Seven Mountains of Borrain could she have survived out there? How long has she been in the jungle?"

"Only two days so far. But now she's gotten herself into a bit of trouble and has been captured by slave traders."

CHAPTER 14

The Procedure Was a Resounding Success

Zhenna almost jumped out of her seat. "*What?* You need to…" She took a moment to pull herself together. "Our briefing didn't say anything about a slave trade among the natives."

"That's another thing we were unaware of. It's extremely difficult to study these peoples in-depth whilst remaining hidden. We will need to study this further now that we're aware of it."

She nodded, looking somewhat calmer.

Dr Aimery put a hand on her arm. "Please understand that although the situation seems bleak, the slave traders offer food and protection from the creatures in the jungle and it is safer for her to stay with them than be alone."

I relaxed a fraction. That made a lot of sense.

"We are also trying to locate Janssen." I tensed again. "We have a Finder here at the base, but he is only Rated as a T6, which means he can't locate people over great distances. He has also been ill and has only recently joined the search team for Tamisan."

I'd heard of the Finders. It was amazing how they could locate objects and people with their minds. It would be interesting to see one in action.

Dr Aimery fidgeted with the Palm-pad on his desk. "Starrick is searching for Tamisan too, so we need to find him and stop him. The jungle is extremely dense and it will be too difficult to search from the air, and of course, we're supposed to be observing the natives unseen. Cloaking a ship doesn't mask the sound of the engines."

He paused and I let it all sink in, but when I looked at him, I could see he wasn't finished.

"There is another thing we've discovered." He looked at me again and I tensed. "The Talent that you have suddenly manifested within the last few days? It was actually transferred from Tamisan's mind to yours without the transfer of consciousness. According to the records, the procedure was a resounding success."

"What?"

He repeated himself, but it wasn't necessary. I'd heard him; I'd just had trouble believing it.

It made sense when I thought about it. Besides it not being common on Shakira, Talent usually manifested around puberty, so I'd thought I was a late bloomer at age twenty-one.

"He transferred only the parts of the brain that contain the psychic abilities and the records show that this was a significant breakthrough in his research and experimentation. The potential is enormous for this kind of procedure. I'd say more than his original Eibhlin Process. Imagine how many people would pay to receive your abilities. All that is needed afterward is some training to control it. He thinks this could make him a very rich man and is confident that it wouldn't be outlawed because it doesn't wipe out anyone's mind. And I'm afraid he is probably right about that part."

So I was Starrick's big success. That did *not* sit well with me. It was hard enough to learn to control my abilities in a short period of time. Now I'd been told it was the result of a reckless bunch of experiments, most of which went horribly wrong.

I clenched my jaw. How dare they do this to us? The urge to punch someone or throw something across the room surged through me.

I heard a crash and turned to see a Palm-pad fall to the floor in the corner.

My eyes snapped to Dr Aimery. "Oh. Apologies. I think that might have been me."

"Try to calm yourself, dear," he said gently. "I know this is all very upsetting. We will need to continue your training as soon as possible so you can learn control."

I nodded as the heat rose in my cheeks. What else could I say?

Dr Aimery straightened his shoulders and someone retrieved the Palm-pad from off the floor for him.

"I think that's enough for today. We will let you know more as we find out more. Go and get something to eat and try to relax. We will need full statements from you all later and we'll record the interviews for our records."

Once we'd been taken to a cafeteria and were able to grab some food, we sat at a table and talked about what Dr Aimery had told us. I was too wound up, but I forced myself to eat because I knew my body needed the nourishment.

Zhenna ran a hand through her hair. "I can't believe this has happened."

Mosuti clenched his fork a little too tightly. "Starrick has a lot to answer for."

"It's just too weird. There's two of me."

"Yes. It's hard to imagine. There were two of me and two of Larissa for a short time, but surely they could have done more instead of just killing them. That's abhorrent and just wrong."

I thought about how terrible it must have been to be thrown into Bazeelia's body and the thoughts to be jumbled up in my mind. Did they give her an injection or just shoot her like they did to the others when the teams from Jannali arrived?

They probably shot her. Me. That would be Starrick's style. Forget being humane or honourable. We were only lab rats anyway. Now I was the one holding my fork too firmly. I made an effort to relax my hand.

Zhenna bit her lip. "I hope Janssen is okay."

My chest tightened. It was too much to hope for. I didn't want to be thinking about this. I couldn't hope.

"I hope he's still alive," Mosuti said. "You saw how dense that jungle was, yes?"

I remembered very well. I pushed food around on my plate and tried to keep calm. "I remember reading the files on all the deadly creatures in the jungle."

Why did I bring that up? That was the last thing I wanted to think about.

Zhenna nodded. "Some of those things are truly terrifying, like the thing that swooped down out of the trees at us."

I shuddered. "Zhenna, your other half is out there in that jungle too."

Chapter 15
Oh, I Do Care

Zhenna cringed, then nodded again. "Other half. That sounds weird."

Mosuti took a sip of his drink. "This is going to take a long time to get used to."

I tried to push my emotions down. I had to be stronger than this. I was letting it get to me. I couldn't afford to hope that Janssen would be found alive and well. If it turned out that he'd been... that he hadn't made it, I was sure my heart would never recover.

Now I knew how much I'd let my guard down when it came to Janssen. He'd somehow gotten past all my defences, and even though I'd run from him after we'd kissed, he was still affecting my heart.

Zhenna put a hand on my arm. "Are you okay?"

I sucked in a deep breath and nodded. "Yes. It's just a lot to take in."

"You got that right."

I had to get out of here the first chance I got. I'd already been planning it, but if the people back home on Shakira thought I was dead, they would have been organizing to sell the house Gran had left to me. I needed to stop them.

I put down my fork and looked at each of them. "I don't know about you two, but I want out. I was trying to get Starrick to transfer me here so I could quit — he'd said he wasn't the person to see to hand in my resignation, that it had to be Doctor Aimery. After everything that's happened, I just want to go home. But I also don't want to leave while Janssen and Tamisan are still out there. I wish there was a way I could help find Janssen."

"Yes. Me too," Mosuti said. "I'm guessing they won't let us do anything to help though."

I sighed. "No." I knew we'd have to leave it to the professionals, but it didn't stop me feeling useless. "Maybe we could delay leaving till they're found."

They nodded, but both told me they wanted to get back to their home planets as soon as they could. Mosuti had quite a large family he wanted to reunite with. Zhenna was a clone from Earth and didn't have a family, but still had two friends who were like family waiting for her. We'd been told that funerals had been organized for each of us, but our caskets hadn't arrived back on our respective planets yet. I was curious to know what was in them.

I shuddered.

How could they do that? How could they lie about our deaths? Did they think they'd get away with it? Surely whatever was in those boxes would be analyzed and found to be fake.

It didn't surprise me that I hadn't been the only one asking to go home.

Zhenna sighed. "What happens to the other me when she's found? If she thinks she's me, she'd want to go home too."

I nodded. "Good question. There can only be one Zhenna Rhodarma, so she'd have to go by the name she made up for herself, I guess."

"Yes. I don't know how all of that will work."

"Doctor Aimery will have some work to do sorting that out."

I kept thinking of the families of the other crew members that hadn't survived. Their loved-ones were still gone. People were grieving right now because of Starrick and his team of doctors.

Zhenna's mind was in the body of some alien woman and had been captured by other aliens from this barbaric world. And Janssen might be alive. Maybe.

I thought about the man I'd accidentally killed. I knew those men would have killed me if I hadn't defended myself. I knew I couldn't have let them shoot me. But I'd promised myself I would never take a life.

All of this was wrong on so many levels.

I clenched my fists.

Mosuti looked down at my hands. "Careful, Larissa. Remember what happened the last time you got angry."

I relaxed my hands. "Oh, yes. Apologies. I forgot."

He smiled gently. "It takes a bit of practice, but you'll get the hang of it eventually. Give it time."

"Thanks."

"It's not that bad, is it?"

I thought about it. "No. In fact, it's quite amazing. Just scary when things fly across the room."

"You'll get it soon. Don't worry."

I wondered who I'd get as a trainer. I hoped that whoever it was, they were actually qualified.

The following morning, I was introduced to the man who was going to give me some real lessons on how to use telekinesis. I was excited to be learning from a Kinetic.

Dr Aimery's smile was contagious. "This is Braydac Novak and he's a T1 in telepathy and telekinesis. He will be able to help you gain control of your ability."

We said our greetings and were ushered into a small room with a table and two uncomfortable-looking chairs.

Once the doctor had left us to it, I smiled down at Braydac. "Thank you for agreeing to teach me."

He crossed his arms, a frown appearing on his handsome face. "Wasn't my idea. I'm no teacher."

What? "So, why are you here?"

"Because the boss told me to teach you control."

I made a move to leave. "You don't have to teach me if you don't want to. I'll find Doctor Aimery. They can get someone else."

He let out a huff. "Sit down. There's no one else. Usually, Darion Andiyar would have done it, but he's out in the jungle looking for that Tamisan girl."

My stomach sank a little. That was Zhenna out there. One of them, anyway. I tried again to imagine her wandering through the jungle. I'd seen her freaking out about the crawling insects when we were looking for specimens right before the attack.

I took a deep breath as I sat. "Have they had any luck yet?"

His eyebrows drew downwards. "How should I know?"

I resisted the urge to roll my eyes. This man had no principles. He reminded me of Starrick. "I was just asking."

This was ridiculous. How could I learn anything from someone who clearly would rather be anywhere else?

I stood. "Don't worry about it. I'll just practice what little I know and get Mosuti to help as much as he can."

He sighed heavily. "Sit down. Just 'cause I don't wanna do it, doesn't mean I won't."

I shifted my weight and crossed my arms. "I'd rather have someone who actually cares whether I learn some control or not."

He narrowed his eyes. "Oh, I *do* care."

"Don't give me that crap."

He leaned forward. "I do. I don't want you to be out of control and give the Normies another reason to fear and hate us."

CHAPTER 16

Show Me What You Got

I huffed and lowered myself back into the chair. "Okay, but you don't have to be an arsehole about it. Just tell me what I need to do."

He ran a hand through his hair and sighed again. "Okay." He leaned his elbows on the table. "So, how much do you know?"

"Almost nothing. The guy who was training me at Maztec was only a Telepath, so he could only guess at how to use telekinesis. I only managed to lift a cup before they started shooting people over there."

I shuddered as the man's blackened chest and vacant stare flashed through my mind.

"That's pretty good considering you had a clueless teacher."

I raised my eyebrows. "Is it? I have no idea how all this works."

"You'll work it out soon. You'll do okay."

I wasn't so sure.

He took a deep breath and rubbed his hands together. "So, let's get down to business. Show me what you got."

"I'm not sure if I can do it just like that."

He didn't break eye contact. "Try."

"Okay." I looked around. "What can I use?"

That was smart — to organize my training and have nothing to use for that training.

Braydac pulled a personal Com out of his pocket. "You can start with this."

"What if I drop it?"

"They're pretty tough. It'll be right."

"Okay."

I took a deep breath and tried to relax and remember everything Conleth had said. It had only been a couple of days, but it seemed like a week since I'd lifted that cup.

I tried a few times without success and sighed. Why wouldn't it work?

Maybe because I was nervous being watched by someone who actually knew how to do it. It was like being judged on a piece of artwork by a seasoned artist.

"Don't sigh. Relax. Concentrate."

"I am."

"You're not relaxed. Stop frowning. Take a few deep breaths. I'm not gonna say anything if you can't do it right. I'm not gonna judge. Pretend I'm not here."

"It's not that easy. I can't remember what Conleth told me about how to draw out my power."

So much had happened since then.

"Okay, you need to be able to search for the power within you and bring it out. It usually feels like it's in the vicinity of your chest. Find it and push it outward. Push it down your arm and into your hand. Then you can use it to move the Com."

That was what I'd done to move the cup. I closed my eyes and concentrated. There it was, deep in my chest. I slowly pulled it out of its hiding place and pushed it down my arm and out toward the Com. I only meant to move it across the table, but it slid right off and Braydac caught it before it could hit the floor.

He actually smiled. "That's better. Now do it again."

Braydac had ended our lesson before lunch, so I was able to grab a bite to eat.

Afterward, I'd been taken to the Medical Facility for a checkup. After my time at Maztec, each checkup made me uneasy.

The nurse was bright and bubbly, despite her dark hair and dark eyes. "'Ello, beautiful girl."

I tried to smile, but I think it came across as a grimace. "Hi."

"I'm Abbi. I'll be your nurse for the afternoon." She covered her mouth as she laughed at her own joke.

I couldn't help the smile that crept across my face as she sent the Bio-scan on its way.

"Do you 'ave any injuries from your ordeal, love?"

"No."

"Any other... issues?" She looked into my eyes intently.

"What kind of issues?"

Her perfectly shaped eyebrows went up. "Some people 'ave trouble with traumatic situations, see. Do you feel like you need to talk to someone?"

"No. I'm okay."

"You're sure?"

I looked into her eyes to reinforce what I was saying. "Yes. Thank you."

"That's good then."

She continued with her examination and checked the report from the Bio-scan. "It all looks good, love."

I was preparing to leave, but she continued reading the data for a while, then turned to me with wide eyes. "You 'eard about what's goin' on out there in the jungle?"

"You mean with the search for Tamisan?"

"Yes. Oh, it's *so* romantic. Darion has never met this girl, but 'e's goin' all out to find her. At the same time, 'e's been in constant contact with 'er through telepathy, helping 'er navigate the dangers of the jungle."

I hadn't considered that telepathy could be used for communication in an emergency. Now that I had these abilities, I needed to find out as much as I could about them.

"She told 'im there's slavers out there," she continued. "We didn't know that. Maybe it's a new thing. Those beast-like men are new. We've been 'ere a while and never seen 'em before."

"Yes. Doctor Aimery told us." *Wait a minute.* "Beast-like men?"

She leaned closer and lowered her voice. "Yep. They look like Primitive Man from Earth — or monkeys. Real ugly. And hairy. They're the ones capturin' people and puttin' 'em in chains. It's awful."

The picture she'd painted in my mind was pretty gruesome.

She flipped her ponytail over her shoulder. "It's 'ard to learn stuff about their cultures and traditions when you 'ave to do it unseen. It don't work real good. We really need someone who can get among the natives without them knowin' we're from another planet."

"Yes. He mentioned that too."

"We have rules about not contactin' or interferin', but I think she broke 'em all." She chuckled. "She didn't mean it, o' course, but what can you do?"

"Not much now, I suppose. We'll just have to get her out of there as quickly as possible."

"Yeah." She tapped on the Palm-pad for a while. "So this poor girl was captured by that maniac, Dr Starrick, and now she's stuck in that jungle all alone. I don't know 'ow she can stand it. 'Ave you seen the pictures of them creatures out there? They're as scary as your worst nightmare, I tell ya. One even looks like a T-Rex from Earth. Some can fly and there's snakes too. No way I could cope. I'd sit in the shade of one of them giant trees, rockin' and mumblin' to meself."

I knew most of this stuff, but I didn't think I'd be able to stop her from telling me about it.

"Yeah, so, it's so romantic, like I said. 'E's searchin' for her. Guidin' her. Keeping 'er from bein' too terrified and promising 'e's gonna find 'er like a knight in shinin' armour in some kiddie story." She sighed. "It's just so..."

"Romantic?"

"Yes." She turned to me. "I wish I had someone like that willin' to risk 'is own skin to come save me. 'E could die out there, but 'e's doin' it anyways. They say that Talents fall in love faster than us 'cause they can read minds, and some of 'em can feel each other's emotions, so I reckon they're probably in love already, even though they never met yet."

She sighed again.

My first thought was that she was silly for thinking like that, but there was something tugging at my heart. To have someone so dedicated to finding me or helping me in such a terrible situation... it made my heart flutter.

The flutter morphed into an ache and I pushed all the emotions down that were threatening to come to the surface. I would *not* be weak.

CHAPTER 17
I Have Something to Tell You

After another two days of Talent training and meetings with Dr Aimery and other people involved with the investigation, we were told that Tamisan had been rescued from the jungle.

Dr Aimery met us in the briefing room in the evening to let us know more about it and we exchanged greetings as we seated ourselves at the table.

He remained standing and held a Palm-pad in front of him. "It's a long story. First of all, she is okay and only has minor injuries. Apparently her body heals itself quickly, so she'll recover in no time."

Zhenna leaned forward. "Can we see her?"

"She's resting at the moment, but I've organized a briefing for tomorrow morning. You'll be able to see her then." He looked at each of us. "You need to know that she is unaware that anyone survived, and before you say anything, we decided not to tell her because we needed her to stay strong and stay focused on getting out of her situation. It was traumatic enough without her worrying about all of you and the fact that Janssen is still out there. She can get a good night's sleep now and we plan to give her the information a piece at a time at the briefing to give her a chance to digest it all."

No one protested. It was a wise decision. Things had been hard enough for me in my situation.

Dr Aimery finally sat down. "Since we last updated you, Tamisan was sold to a native, then escaped and met up with Darion and his team in the jungle. Starrick's team somehow managed to find them and attempted to capture the whole team and Starrick tried to shoot Darion, but they were stopped and have all been arrested and brought back here."

Zhenna gripped the table with both hands. "I hope Starrick gets put away for life for what he's done."

"I'm sure the court will not be lenient, my dear, with Doctor Starrick or his associates. They've broken several laws, ended lives and ruined many others."

There were a few choice words amongst us regarding what we all thought of Starrick and anyone who worked with him.

Dr Aimery stood and ended our meeting, saying that someone would fetch us in the morning and we would meet Tamisan and Darion.

⊷✦⊶

The next morning, we were ushered into a small room down the hall from the briefing room and asked to wait till we were called in to see Tamisan. We'd been told that Mosuti would be called first, then me, and Zhenna would only be called if Tamisan thought she could handle it.

My nerves were getting the better of me while we waited to see what would happen in the briefing room. How would Tamisan take the news? How was she dealing with everything that had happened to her?

Zhenna started pacing the room, her red shipsuit showing off her curves as she walked. "Do you think she'll want to see me?"

Mosuti smiled. "Would *you* want to see you?"

She stopped. "Yes, of course, but—"

"Then you have your answer."

"But she's not me anymore. Sort of. They said she's changed."

"Yes, but I'm sure she'll want to see you."

She frowned. "It's gonna be weird if she does want to speak to me. I'll be talking to myself."

I tapped a fingernail on the table. "I hope she wants to see all of us."

Mosuti smiled. "She will."

We talked some more about what might happen, but decided all we could do was wait and see.

After my second cup of coffee, a popular beverage from Earth that I'd discovered since I arrived at Jannali, they called Mosuti into the briefing room.

My heart pounded as he leapt out of his seat and followed the woman out of the room.

Zhenna and I looked at each other and she gave me a wobbly smile.

"I hope she's okay," Zhenna said for the fifth time.

I just smiled.

It seemed like an eternity before the door swished open and the woman stepped in again. "Larissa?"

I sat up straighter. "Yes?"

"Come with me, please."

I stood and followed her, looking back once to see Zhenna's hopeful face.

"It'll be okay," I sent to her. *"She'll want to see you, too."*

She tried a smile, but didn't quite get there. *I hope so*, she thought.

My legs were jelly as I walked to the briefing room. How would she react? What should I do?

This would be weird for both of us.

I tried to compose myself. The door opened and my gaze swept the room as it occurred to me that I had no idea what Tamisan looked like. My eyes were drawn to a short woman with long, black hair and eyes almost as dark as a Shakiran's as she stared back at me with a hopeful expression. She sucked in a breath and tears filled her eyes as I walked in.

This is Zhenna.

I kept repeating it, hoping it would sink in.

She looked so different. I felt for her. To her, I was still the friend that she'd thought was dead, so even though it was a bit awkward, I gave her a hug to show her that it was okay. That I was still here for her.

She was so short; the size of a twelve-year-old Shakiran.

This is Zhenna. This is Zhenna.

She would be confused and afraid.

We both cried for a while, but I had to see her face. I stepped back and had a good look at her. This Althari woman was beautiful with her long, black hair and intense brown eyes and shapely body. It was hard to believe Zhenna's mind was in this body, as well as being out in the other room.

"Zhenna? Is it really you?" I blurted.

It was a silly thing to say under the circumstances, but my mind was struggling to comprehend.

There was only a ghost of a smile as her bottom lip trembled. "Yes, it's me. I'm only different on the outside."

"You're even shorter now," I said. Of all the things racing around in my head, why did I say that? I hoped she wasn't offended.

I glanced around the room at all the eager faces watching us to see how this would go and to see how Zhenna — I mean Tamisan — was handling it.

It must have been difficult for her. So much more than it had been for Zhenna, Mosuti, and I. Nothing had turned out the way we'd expected it to. We were supposed to be working for Voyager Division studying these natives, not *becoming* one of them.

That made me think of the abilities that had been transferred from her mind.

"I have something to tell you..." Her eyebrows shot up in alarm, so I quickly continued. "Starrick experimented on me too and gave me psychic abilities like yours." She gasped. "He didn't tell me what they'd done, but once the people from Jannali raided Maztec, the records they found showed that they'd actually transferred the Talent from your mind to mine, without transferring your consciousness with it."

I hoped I hadn't told her more than Dr Aimery wanted me to, but I needn't have worried. He explained that Starrick and his doctors had recorded extra activity outside the normal areas of the brain while she was hooked up to the EEG. They assumed that it was the part of the brain that contained the psychic abilities, so they mapped it and transferred it to my mind.

"I didn't know what was happening and needed some training. Someone at Maztec gave me some basic lessons and Mosuti has helped since I got here..."

I wasn't sure whether to mention that I was a Kinetic too. Maybe I could tell her later. I didn't want to overwhelm her even more, especially since she didn't know about Zhenna yet.

Mosuti and I told her about what had happened when the soldiers from Jannali arrived and that Starrick was out looking for her at the time. When we told her Starrick had given the order to kill us all, she cringed, so I assumed she was hearing it for the first time.

"I knew their intentions before they even opened my door," Mosuti said. "I exerted some pressure on their minds as soon as they barged in so they couldn't move. I slipped out of the room and locked the door. Then I released them and heard them fall to the floor."

I imagined them falling like marionettes after having their strings cut.

"I'd only just managed to lift a cup in my last lesson," I added, "so I didn't know what to do. I could hear the commotion and heard screaming. Heard them getting closer. I picked up the little table in my room, ready to charge at whoever came in through the door. I didn't know what to expect and just hoped for the best."

I told her how I'd barged at the men as they entered and how the man behind had ended up being shot. I said I couldn't look at the dead man, but that was a lie. I'd had a good, long look. I'll never forget his face as long as I live.

CHAPTER 18

Such a Disgusting and Dishonourable Thing

My nails were digging into my palms and I tried to stop myself from clenching my fists so hard. "I didn't know where I was or which way to go, but then I found Mosuti. I couldn't believe he was alive."

It occurred to me that I'd told Tamisan about my kinetic abilities by mentioning the cup.

Mosuti ran a hand through his hair. "We found a place to hide until the soldiers from Jannali found us."

Tamisan frowned. "Starrick is crazy. He thought he could do this to us and get away with it."

We both nodded. What kind of person would do this and not have a problem with causing so many deaths?

I unclenched my sore hands again and tried to relax. I did *not* want to lose control in front of all these people. Braydac may have been without honour, but he was right about not needing to give Normals a reason to hate us.

I needed to keep practicing control.

I forced myself to smile. "I'm going to start formal training for my Talent once I get back home to Shakira."

Tamisan smiled too. "That's great."

It was still hard to believe this was Zhenna. I thought about the last time I saw her before the attack, which brought Janssen to my mind. Again.

I frowned. "I'm hoping they will find Janssen soon."

"I hope he's alright. The jungle is a dangerous place to be." Then she added, "But I think he will have a better chance of avoiding trouble than I did. It's definitely not a good place for a female on her own!"

"You're not wrong." I tried to imagine her wandering through the underbrush. Then I tried to imagine Janssen trudging through the same foliage with vines hanging down and — I had to stop myself. I needed to get control of my emotions. "I wish... I should have told him I liked him..."

Why did I say that when I hadn't told anyone what had happened between Janssen and I?

I think maybe I'd been ashamed of my lack of self-control. I'd lost control when he kissed me like that... when I'd eagerly returned his kisses...

"Don't beat yourself up about it. You didn't know."

None of us could have predicted this mess.

I suppressed a shudder. "I thought we'd have a chance to get to know each other while we worked."

I needed to stop talking about Janssen before I lost control of my emotions and my Talent.

She gave me a sad smile. "Me too."

I pushed down my pain so I wouldn't cry and somehow forced myself to smile. "I would like to catch up with you later on – after I finish my first semester of training maybe."

"I'd like that very much," she said as she turned to Mosuti. "I'd like to catch up with you too, Mosuti."

"Yes, of course," he replied, waving a hand to include both of us.

"Maybe you can teach us more about how to use our Talent," Tamisan suggested.

"Oh, yes. There is much for you both to learn..." he said, his smile turning into a smirk.

Tamisan and I nodded.

She looked from me to Mosuti. "So, did they tell you everyone was dead, like they did to me?"

"Yes," I said, and Mosuti nodded.

"They fed me some garbage about contacting relatives and sending bodies back home to Earth and the others' home planets." She pursed her lips together. "They must have sent back ashes or something. Told them all that we were burned to death, or some other rubbish."

It was such a disgusting and dishonourable thing to do. And to add to that injustice, our friends and relatives would now be told that we were still alive, while the others would find out that the nature of their loved-one's death was a lie.

At least Zhenna and Mosuti would be going home to friends and family. There would be no one waiting for me and Voyager Division probably had no idea what they were going to do with Tamisan.

"What happens with me?" Tamisan asked Dr Aimery. "Will you tell my friends what happened? I mean, I'm not even me anymore, so I don't know how that would work."

"Well." He paused for a few seconds. "That is one thing we must decide on. But first, there is something else we need to tell you."

She was silent for a while, but she was looking at the man who'd come to stand by her side. I was sure they were having a telepathic conversation. This must have been Darion. I'd heard so much about him from Abbi over the last few days that I felt almost like I knew him.

She turned back to Dr Aimery. "What is it?"

He took a slow breath. "You might want to sit down."

She frowned. "No, I'm good."

I couldn't help thinking she should've taken his advice.

He cleared his throat, probably trying to find the right words. "Okay. You – ah, Zhenna – was not terminated like the records show. We found her at Maztec. She was rescued too."

Tamisan sucked in a breath. "What...?"

"She is here, waiting for my signal like the others. Just say the word and I will send her in."

Her face went pale.

"Are you okay?" Darion asked.

Mosuti stepped forward. "Breathe, Tamisan."

She took some deep breaths, but started to sway. Darion was there in an instant to guide her back into her seat.

She looked up at Dr Aimery. "Can I see her?"

"Are you sure?" Darion asked. "I thought you were going to faint..."

"I'm okay," she assured him. "I have to see her."

I couldn't stop the smile spreading across my face. I knew she'd say yes. Zhenna would be elated.

Dr Aimery used a Com unit on the table to ask for Zhenna to be brought in. She walked in a few seconds later, smiling nervously.

Tamisan stood and her movements were unsure, but Zhenna only hesitated for a second. "Hello."

Silence fell as they stared at each other and everyone waited to see what they would do.

Tamisan was taking shallow breaths, but managed a "hello." Then she said, "This is going to sound kinda strange, but it's good to see you!"

Zhenna's smile widened. "It's really good to see you, too. Are you really me? I know they told me what happened, but I still can't believe it!"

Tamisan's eyes welled up. "Yes. I'm you, but I'm me. I'm kind of different now. It's hard to explain."

Zhenna went to speak, but no words came out, so she closed her mouth, running a hand nervously through her hair.

"I can't believe you're still alive!" Tamisan told her. "Starrick told me my body was badly burned and I was clinically dead, and that's why they transferred my – your – our – consciousness into this body."

CHAPTER 19

I Know How Much it Means for You to Have it Back

Everyone in the room would be struggling to process this. It was the strangest thing I'd ever witnessed.

Zhenna straightened. "Yes, well, as you can see, I'm still here and very much alive. My life – your life – wasn't in any danger. I had a splitting headache when I woke up, and all my muscles were stiff and sore from the stunner blast."

I grimaced at the memory. If I never experienced a stunner blast again, I'd be happy.

Zhenna sighed. "He didn't tell me about you or any of the others. The 'everybody is dead except you' story seems to be the one he told to every single one of us. I don't know how he pulled it off, though. I didn't see anyone else the whole time I was there. When I was taken to the lab or Medical Facility, there was never anyone else in sight."

That must have taken some careful planning. Maztec wasn't very big, and I was sure there was only one Medical Facility.

Tamisan ran her fingers through her hair, which I recognised as something Zhenna did when she was nervous or stressed. "Yeah. Same here. I managed to zap the lock on my room with static electricity and went for a walk around. I found a man with Mosuti's mind scrambled up in his head. That was scary. I even found a Vid, but couldn't access anything. I was caught on camera doing it and Starrick gave me a bit of a roasting over it." She cringed. "Starrick wasn't happy."

Zhenna nodded. "Starrick wasn't happy when you ran away."

"Yeah. Mosuti told me. I managed to get away, but got myself into some worse trouble. The jungle was so horrible..."

Zhenna nodded. "Yes, they told me."

Tamisan seemed to be deep in thought. She shuddered, then tears filled her eyes and rolled down her cheeks.

Darion was there for her again. "What is it?"

My mind ran through all the things Abbi had told me about him. She was right. I could sense the connection between them.

Tamisan turned away. "I'm sorry. It's just that I realized that... Z-Zhenna will be going home to my... her friends... and..."

She turned into Darion and he wrapped her in a comforting embrace. "Shhh... It will be alright."

My heart went out to her, but also ached for the love I could feel coming from both of them. I longed for that feeling... it was all I'd ever wanted...

Wait — how could I feel their emotions?

Wasn't empathy another psychic ability?

I sucked in a breath. Tamisan had to be an Empath too. It must have been transferred with her other abilities.

Zhenna put an arm around Tamisan. "I feel bad that I'll get to see Oliana and Kaliya again and you can't."

She and Darion comforted Tamisan while she sobbed quietly.

Zhenna rubbed a hand over Tamisan's back. It was strange because it was like she was comforting herself. "When I woke up at Maztec, Starrick told me all his lies. I believed him, but knew something was wrong when he wouldn't let me out of the room by myself. I couldn't do anything about it. He did the usual testing on me and when the raid started, I could hear the commotion outside. The soldiers from Jannali found me before Starrick's men and they took me back here. I was amazed when I found out all the things that have happened to you."

Tamisan finally pulled herself together. "It isn't all bad. I have these abilities now, and they are amazing. Do you remember when Mosuti showed you – me – us how to have a conversation using telepathy and we wondered what it would be like to be able to send thoughts back to him?" Zhenna nodded. "Well, it's even more incredible than we imagined!"

It was weird hearing her talk like that. It would definitely take a while to get used to.

As I watched the different expressions play out on their faces, I wondered if they were having a telepathic conversation.

We told Tamisan we'd spent some time together since we'd arrived at Jannali and that they'd told us what had happened to her in the jungle.

I kept wondering what she was going to do now. What could she do if Zhenna was going back home to Earth? She wouldn't be able to go back to her life. "Hey, Zhenna."

"Yes?" they both answered in unison, then started to giggle.

I heard a couple of other giggles around the room.

Tamisan turned to me. "Call me Tamisan. That will avoid confusion."

I couldn't help smiling. "Uh, yeah. Okay. So, what are you going to do now?"

"Umm. I don't really know. I'm still trying to get my head around everything." She was quiet for a while, deep in thought, then turned to Zhenna. "Could you do me a favour? When you go home, could you organize to send me copies of all of our photos, please?"

"Yes, of course!" Zhenna replied. Tears welled up in her eyes again.

Tamisan smiled and thanked her.

Zhenna sniffed. "They recovered our stuff from the Outrider and I thought you might like to have this…"

She removed the locket on a chain that she'd always worn around her neck and gave it to Tamisan. Tamisan choked back a sob. It must have meant a great deal to her.

Her eyes widened. "Wait. They gave you stuff from the Outrider?"

Zhenna frowned. "Yes, but only about half–"

"They gave me half too. The *other* half."

"To keep the lies going, I guess…"

I clenched my fists. Starrick didn't care about the trauma he'd caused with his disgusting experiments.

Tamisan's cheeks were soaked with tears. "Thank you…" she whispered.

"It won't replace all that you've lost," Zhenna told her as she put the necklace around her neck, "but I know how much it means for you to have it back…"

They embraced and tears streamed freely down my cheeks. I looked around. There wasn't a dry eye in the room.

⸻◆⸻

We were finally going home.

Later that afternoon, we'd been told we would be leaving for Earth the next day. It seemed both too soon and not soon enough.

We'd voiced our concerns about leaving Tamisan so soon and Janssen still lost in the jungle, but Dr Aimery told us the Acronis was heading back to Earth for supplies, which meant we'd be here for at least another month if we didn't board the ship in the morning. Then add the two weeks of travel time.

Zhenna and Mosuti couldn't afford to take six weeks to get back to their friends and family and I had to get back to Shakira. I'd been in contact with the authorities and found out my great aunt had put in a claim on the house. I could bet all the credits in my account that she would be trying anything she could to keep the house she thought she'd be inheriting once my funeral was over with.

She was my grandfather's sister and she and the rest of his family had disowned him after he'd married a Taonese woman and not a Shakiran. I planned to have a will drawn up as soon as I arrived home so that they wouldn't be entitled to anything.

I wasn't exactly thinking straight after losing Gran and didn't think to organize a will before I left, but after coming close to dying, I wasn't going to leave all the legalities to chance any longer.

We'd had enough time to pack, eat and shower, and had twenty minutes to get to the place where we'd be teleported aboard the Outrider. I wasn't sure how I'd feel about being on that ship again, or the Acronis, but it was the only way to get off this rock and back to Shakira.

Abbi approached us in the hallway as we followed a soldier to our destination. "'Ello, beautiful people, 'ave you 'eard the news?"

Mosuti stopped and I almost walked into him. "What news?"

CHAPTER 20

I'd Found Someone Who Could Break My Heart

"It's about Tamisan. And that Doctor Starrick."

"What about them?"

"Well, 'e got away last night, didn't 'e? Found Tamisan, drugged 'er, an' tried to blow the whole base up. She stopped 'im an' that, but they don't know how bad she's been affected by this drug that s'posed ta block Talent. They have ta wait till she wakes up."

We all fired questions at her.

"The doctors reckon she'll be okay soon enough, but it was scary. Didn't anyone tell ya?"

We looked at the soldier who'd been taking us to the teleport point.

"Don't look at me. Just following orders. I wasn't given permission to tell you anything."

I frowned at him. "Don't you think we should have been told before we flew back to the other side of the Known Universe?"

"Yeah, but it wasn't my job. I expected that someone would tell you when we got to the teleport point."

I sighed. I understood how military personnel had to follow orders.

Abbi spoke quickly and I had to concentrate to keep up. She didn't know how Starrick had escaped, but he'd somehow knocked out the guard who was posted outside Darion's quarters and got to Tamisan. He stuck a needle into her neck, which was supposed to paralyze her and block her Talent, but she'd somehow managed to keep moving. He'd gone to the Generator Room and tried to cause it to overload and explode, which would have destroyed the whole base, but she stopped the overload.

Starrick had been shot and killed and Tamisan was still recovering.

I had an overwhelming urge to see her.

Zhenna had the same idea. "Can we see her? I need to see her and make sure she's okay."

"I'm not sure if they'd let ya in, but you could try."

The soldier put his hands up. "No can do. Sorry, but the shuttle isn't gonna wait for any of you. It's due to fly outta here in—" he looked at his wrist, "—seven minutes and you need to be on it."

Zhenna's eyes welled up, but she knew she couldn't risk missing the flight. None of us could.

We had to go.

Abbi followed us to the teleport point where we met with Dr Aimery and Braydac and I realized Braydac was the one who would be teleporting us. What other abilities did he have?

They greeted us and the doctor told us the same story we'd heard from Abbi. No one mentioned that she'd already told us in case she wasn't meant to say anything.

Dr Aimery cleared his throat. "I am so sorry your employment with us didn't turn out the way it was supposed to. Doctor Starrick may not be here to answer for his crimes, but we will be prosecuting those involved with his illegal experimentation, you can be sure of that."

That only made me feel a teeny bit better.

We said our goodbyes, Dr Aimery and Abbi wished us luck, and we were told to hold Braydac's hands while he teleported us to the Outrider. He disappeared again once he'd made sure we were settled.

Memories swarmed around me as I looked at the seat where Janssen had strapped himself in for the trip down to the surface what seemed like years ago.

I forced myself to look away. I had to be strong.

The pilot ran some checks and made sure we were strapped in correctly before taking off.

The G-forces kept me glued to my seat and the ship rumbled and shuddered until we'd cleared the atmosphere. Then we seemed to glide over to the Acronis. Once we'd docked, we filed out and were shown to our quarters.

There were other people aboard the ship, but I had no intention of getting to know them over the next two weeks. I'd learnt my lesson about letting people into my heart. The ache in my chest confirmed it.

It would take me a long time to bury all of these emotions, but I'd do it.

As we started our journey back, we were offered food and drinks and I tried to pretend that being a couple of rooms away from where I'd gotten to know Janssen wasn't killing me inside.

❖

I'd managed to avoid the hydroponics garden for a full day, but no matter what I did, I was drawn to the room.

I waited till after dinner on the second day and crept in there. I was relieved to see there was no one around. I needed some time alone in here.

I walked past the carrots and tomatoes, closed my eyes and replayed the scene in my head. Janssen and I had been drawn to this room by our interest in plants and we'd gone through each bay, looking at the exotic plants from different parts of the universe. We'd started with the carrots and tomatoes as we were interested in the vegetables from Earth.

We ended up spending so much time in here after that. He was so easy-going and I found it refreshing to talk to a Shakiran that wasn't obsessed with combat training and weapons.

We both understood that other professions besides the military were important. Most Shakiran parents encouraged their children to go into the military, even in times of peace. Choosing a non-military profession was almost considered shameful. I had no idea what my parents would have thought of my career choice, but I knew exactly what my grandfather and brother thought. It hadn't stopped me. And I was still alive. And they weren't. So there was that.

Janssen's family grew food to supply the nearby towns and cities, and also for the military, so he hadn't had any pressure from family to join the fight.

My mind shifted to the last time we'd met in here.

On our last night before reaching Althar 3, we talked about anything and everything and were excited about starting our new jobs on a largely-unexplored planet.

I'd thought that spending time with Janssen and sharing our knowledge of botany wouldn't do any harm. I understood that I'd needed some contact with people after Gran passed, just to get me through it. I thought it would be alright. I could do this to help me get over losing her.

Janssen was pointing out the new flower buds on a plant from Taon and I leaned in to get a better look.

He was close. I could smell his deodorant and his distinct scent. Was it my imagination that I thought he smelled like a certain flower on Shakira?

As I saw the details in each petal, I also saw him in my peripheral vision. He leaned closer still. I turned to face him and he closed the distance between us and searched my face for a few moments. He must have found what he was looking for before pressing his lips to mine.

I sucked in a breath.

I should have pulled away. I should have told him no.

But the rush of sensations running through me and the way my heart thundered in my chest made me forget all those rules I'd set for myself.

Before I knew it, I was wrapping my arms around his neck and pulling him closer. I couldn't get enough of him. His hands on my back lit a fire within me and he slid them down to my hips and back up again.

We kept kissing until Janssen pulled back and wrapped me in his warm embrace. It took a while for our breathing to return to normal.

I'd never been kissed like that before. Sure, I'd kissed a guy at university, but it didn't feel anything like this.

My heart sang and tears welled in my eyes. This was something else.

Janssen pulled back and looked into my eyes. "I hope I wasn't too forward. I've wanted to do that for a long while now."

I smiled and my heart skipped a beat. I didn't know what to say. Maybe I'd wanted him to kiss me and hadn't known it.

He placed small kisses on my cheeks and nose and lips and my heart soared.

I wrapped my arms around him again and put my head on his shoulder. I needed time to process these emotions that were threatening to drown me. They were nothing like anything I'd ever felt.

It was like something had been missing my whole life and I'd finally found it.

Then something clicked. I'd finally found someone I could maybe fall in love with. Someone I could spend my life with. Like Gran and Grandfather. Like Mother and Father.

It was like someone stuck a knife in my heart. I'd found someone who could break my heart into such tiny pieces that I could never recover. When he died — and he would, because everyone else in my life did — I would be so broken. I wouldn't be able to face living.

I couldn't do this. I couldn't let that happen. I had to get out of here. I had to keep away.

I pulled away from him. "I have to go."

He frowned. "What? Why? What's wrong?"

"Nothing. I... I have to go. I have to... think. My apologies!"

And with that, I ran from the room.

My eyes flew open. My cheeks were wet. The tears kept coming and I let them all out. Everything that had happened seemed to overwhelm me and pull me down and I let it. I leaned my back on one of the plant bays and slid down to the floor, pulling my knees up to my chest.

I stayed there for a long time before I ran out of tears. I wasn't sure how late it was, but I managed to get back to my quarters without running into anyone.

I lay in my bunk and pushed all of those dangerous feelings down deep. Locked them away. I had to. I couldn't face the next two weeks if I didn't.

And I vowed not to visit the hydroponics garden again.

CHAPTER 21
I Was Determined Not to Fall Apart

I stood outside my house and tried to calm my pounding heart. I had to face walking through the front door without seeing Gran there to greet me. It wouldn't be as bad as the first time I'd done it, but I still wanted to turn and run.

Thoughts raced through my head. So much had happened since I was here last. So much had changed, but the house looked the same as it always did. The creaky front steps. The covered verandah with the creeping vines. The stained wooden door with the small stained-glass window.

I took a long slow breath.

I wondered how Zhenna and Mosuti were doing. They should have been reunited with their families and friends by now.

Four days into our journey home, we'd received news about Tamisan.

The drug Starrick had given her was meant to block her Talent and paralyze her, but because she wasn't human, the drug didn't work at first. He'd planned to kill her while she was paralyzed and he'd almost succeeded once the drug started to take effect.

As Tamisan had stopped the overload, there had been a flash of light that had damaged her retinas and caused her to become blind, but the doctors were confident that it was only temporary.

Starrick had been shot dead once Jannali personnel had been able to gain access to the Generator Room.

Once Tamisan woke, she could only move her eyes at first, but had started to make a slow recovery.

We'd been shocked by the news — especially Zhenna — but there was nothing we could do.

I'd been surprised at my reaction to Starrick's death. I would normally feel sadness when someone lost their life, but anger swelled within me and I was glad he was dead. He'd caused so much pain and had killed a lot of people for his own gain. He hadn't cared about anyone but himself and his research.

The others felt the same.

By the end of our trip, we'd received an update. Tamisan's paralysis had slowly subsided and she'd recovered the use of her Talent. Her eyesight was the last thing to return. It had been a relief to hear that she was okay. Zhenna had shed some tears. They were the same person after all.

My thoughts returned to the present. I was still staring at the front door. I held my breath. Closed my eyes.

I could do this. I *would* do this.

My heart pounded louder in my ears. I took a deep breath, then let it out slowly. Walking through this door when I'd returned from the university after Gran had died had been soul-crushing. I was determined not to fall apart like that again.

When I opened my eyes, the familiar door beckoned, with the intricate vines growing up around its frame. I turned the handle and my mind could easily imagine Gran walking up to greet me, smiling sweetly.

But she wasn't here. She would never be here again. The house was empty.

As I stepped inside, it was suddenly colder. My mind filled with memories of her and Eli and Grandfather.

My eyes filled with tears as I wandered around the house. I wouldn't cry. I knew what Grandfather would say. Crying was for the weak. And I'd done too much of it lately.

But a sob escaped as I peeked into Eli's room and by the time I reached Gran's, I had totally broken down. Again. I threw myself onto her bed and let my tears flow freely.

I had no one left. No one to talk to about the awful things that had happened to me.

Zhenna and Mosuti had people waiting. People who cared. People who would hug them and comfort them and...

I didn't hold back. I let everything pour out of me.

Afterward, I had the painstaking job of pulling myself together and pushing all the memories and emotions down and hiding them away in the corner of my heart.

There were a few things lying on the floor that had been sitting neatly on shelves when I'd entered the room. I picked them up and returned them to their places. I still needed to learn control when I was emotional.

I needed to decide what to do with the house. If I couldn't stay here without falling to pieces, I had to sell up and move out. I decided that once I'd sorted out the mess with my aunt and her lawyer, I would put this place up for sale.

And I would find my nearest training centre for the Talented.

Four days later, I stood out the front of the Talent Training Centre in Andorra, which was the nearest city. Training centres were rare on Shakira, so it was fortunate that there was one close to me.

I'd spent the last few days going back and forth with my lawyer and my Great Aunt Kutuka's lawyer, proving I wasn't dead and making sure that all the paperwork was in place to prevent any of my grandfather's family from getting my home.

I'd thought long and hard about what I would do with it. Yes, I'd be selling it, but till then, I decided that my cousin, Cassia, would get the house if anything happened to me. And I would change it to include the next property I bought.

Cassia was my father's brother's child. We'd played together often as children before Eli and I were taken to the country to escape the war. She'd been taken out of the city too, and thankfully, her parents had survived the bombings.

We'd kept in touch from time to time in the years since. She was the only relative I would have liked to give the house to.

I stepped inside and focused on the woman behind the desk as I approached her.

She looked up from her computer screen, her eyes so much darker than mine. "Can I help you?"

"I have an appointment with Alorin Dokani," I told her.

Her smile was infectious. "Certainly. Please take a seat."

I hadn't been sitting long before my name was called and I was ushered into a small room with a couple of comfy chairs placed on either side of a small table.

Alorin was tall, even by Shakiran standards, and his hair was only shoulder-length, which was a little unusual. We clasped each other's wrists and he introduced himself as he offered me a seat.

"Please make yourself comfortable."

He began by asking some questions about my family and if I had any relatives with Talent. I could be truthful about that — that was a definite no — and I was mindful that Dr Aimery had told me not to make my situation known as it was a very sensitive issue. No one knew what the public's reaction would be if they knew Talent could be transferred from one mind to another. There would be many people against it and others would be clamouring to have it done.

Then there was the issue of it being done against my will. There would be all sorts of legal problems and tensions between the different planets involved, and we didn't need the public weighing in on that either.

I told Alorin my Talent had manifested unexpectedly at a late age. That should be enough information.

"I was off-world when it happened and I've had some basic training to help me gain some control, but now I need some professional guidance."

His smile widened. "Well, you've come to the right person. I can certainly help you with that."

"I haven't been Rated yet."

"Uh huh. Now, can you tell me which ability you have developed?"

"Telepathy. That one was first." He nodded. "Then a few days later, telekinesis." His eyes widened. "And more recently, I've been able to feel other's emotions sometimes. If they're strong."

It looked like he'd stopped breathing.

"Alorin? Are you okay?"

He seemed to come back to himself. "Yes. So you're telling me you have *three* abilities?"

"Yes. Is there something wrong?"

"No. It's just that it's extremely rare, especially here on Shakira."

What could I say? I couldn't tell him the truth. I hoped he didn't get suspicious.

Then I thought, *suspicious of what? How could anyone in the universe possibly guess what they did to me?*

I took a deep breath. "So what happens now?"

"I can train you in telepathy and telekinesis, but I'm not sure how I can help with the Empathy. We don't have anyone here with that ability. I will find out what we can do for you and get back to you."

I put a smile on my face despite my concern. "Okay."

I'd already had this problem twice.

He told me to relax and we went through some exercises so he could see what level I was at and we discussed the Talents' Code of Conduct. He was happy that I'd read it and knew it pretty well.

When we'd finished, I was feeling much better about it all. Alorin was a professional and had a much better attitude than Conleth and Braydac. Of course, Mosuti didn't have a bad attitude, but we hadn't had much time together and he wasn't a Kinetic.

I'd booked twice-weekly lessons with Alorin and was looking forward to being able to control my abilities, especially the telekinesis. I'd almost thrown a cup across the room when dealing with Great Aunt Kutuka's lawyer. What part about the fact that I wasn't dead didn't they understand?

CHAPTER 22
Our Boss Wants to See You

It had been two weeks since I'd been back at home and I was slowly adjusting to life after being part of a madman's illegal experiments that had changed me forever. I was still haunted by the memories of the attack in the jungle and the vacant stare of the soldier at Maztec, but I was trying to put them behind me. Dwelling on them was not good for me.

I practiced what I'd learned from Alorin by moving various objects around the house and garden with my mind, but there was no one at home to have a telepathic conversation with.

I'd finally received a Talent Rating for telepathy and telekinesis, which was T1 for both. Dr Aimery had told us Tamisan was a strong Talent, so I shouldn't have been surprised. I was excited because having strong abilities would mean I wouldn't be limited in what I could do with them.

They hadn't been able to Rate my level of empathy as there was no one at the centre with that ability and it was a difficult ability to measure. I wasn't concerned about it at that point.

It was the last day of the working week and I was leaving the Training Centre after a night session. It was dark, so I hurried across the car park toward my hovercar. I saw a dark shadow under a bush in the garden to the side of the car park and as I moved closer I could see what appeared to be a messy pile of clothing on the grass. Maybe they were robes. Then I could make out a black hood with blonde hair covering a face. It must have been a child of maybe twelve or fourteen — too small to be an adult Shakiran. I couldn't tell if it was a boy or girl with long hair being common to both on Shakira.

There was no movement. I was frozen in place, unsure what to do.

There was no one else in the car park.

What happened to them? Are they alright? Should I call for help or go over and see if I can help them?

My feet were moving before I'd finished those thoughts and I approached cautiously. "Hello?"

There was still no movement and I strained my eyes to see if I could make out the rise and fall of their breathing, but it was too dark.

I kept an eye on my surroundings as I moved closer.

"Hello? Are you okay?"

Nothing.

"Do you need help?"

Still nothing.

What could have happened to them outside a training centre?

I sank to my knees in the soft grass and pushed the hair aside to see their face. "Can I help—"

A hand flew up and a cold spray wet my face. I jerked my head away and tried to take a defensive stance, but couldn't get my right leg under me properly and stumbled backwards, landing on my backside.

The spray tasted bitter and was in my eyes and mouth and up my nose. I tried to ignore that as I finally got to my feet and could make out three blurry shapes in the dim light. Two short ones and one tall. There was no longer a body lying on the ground.

I sized up my opponents as my vision cleared slightly. Judging by their build, the shorter ones were not children. They were possibly from another planet; no adult Shakirans were that short. I rubbed my eyes quickly and blinked repeatedly, but my vision didn't improve.

The third one was Shakiran. That was easy to see with his height and long blonde hair.

I tried to keep an eye on all three of them as they spread out around me. "What do you want?"

"You," one of the shorter men said, using Basic instead of speaking Shakiran.

"Well, that's obvious, but why?"

"Our boss wants to see you."

I looked around, hoping to find someone to help me. "That's not very helpful."

They continued to move around me, circling me, and I tried to stay alert, but my head started to feel fuzzy. Not a good sign.

Panic gripped me.

What did they spray me with?

The Shakiran stepped closer and I gave him a roundhouse kick to the midsection; he went down like a sack of potatoes. I lashed out at the other two with my fists and they stumbled away from me.

My hands hurt. I hadn't punched anyone or anything in years.

My head spun a little and panic worked its way down the length of my spine. The drug was taking effect quickly. How long could I stay conscious?

I was in trouble.

It seemed easy to fight them off — especially considering the condition I was in — but then a flash of charred flesh and those sightless eyes filled my mind and my knees nearly gave way. I didn't want to hurt anyone. Or kill anyone. Those eyes still haunted me.

The Shakiran got to his feet quickly and they resumed their hovering, no doubt embarrassed by how easily I'd brought them down.

The fuzziness spread throughout my body and I shook my hands, hoping to keep the circulation going.

One of the others spoke up. "He wants you to help him with his research, that's all. We know about what happened to you on Althar 3."

"What?"

My tongue and fingertips started to go numb.

No...

How could they know anything about what had happened on Althar 3? It was being kept quiet. Maybe they were with Voyager Division. Or maybe they were friends of Dr Starrick.

No. I *would not* go back to that base at Maztec.

"We know all about it. We know how you acquired your Talent. He just wants your help and nothing more. Then you will be free to go."

Blackness crowded in at the edges of my vision. I wasn't going to last much longer. "Why not just ask me? Instead of sending you three goons."

"It's not our job to ask why. We just get paid for doing a job. Nothin' personal."

My legs wobbled and I swayed a little. I could hardly see. It didn't matter if I agreed with them or not. They were going to take me anyway. I could see they were biding their time, waiting for me to drop.

It seemed I didn't have a choice. There was no point in arguing with them. They would soon have me.

My sluggish mind was trying to plan ahead. Where would they take me? What would I do once I got there? Did they only want to talk to me? I found that hard to believe.

My terrified mind started to slow even further. I wanted to scream, call for help, but when I opened my mouth, no sound came out. There was nothing I could do. I would have to cooperate when I came to and then try to reason with their boss. I would tell him what he wants to know and be back home...

The ground tilted and came up to meet me as everything went black.

CHAPTER 23
Nothin' Personal

I woke to darkness. The bed was too firm to be my own. Panic sliced into me as the thought that maybe I was back at Maztec entered my mind.

I tried to sit up, but my head pounded and my stomach roiled and I lay back down, waiting for it to settle so I wouldn't throw up.

Where am I?

I couldn't remember anything. There was a small lump on my forehead.

I pushed myself into a sitting position, slowly this time. I fumbled around in the darkness and found a bedside lamp. Flicked it on.

I was in a cabin similar to the ones aboard the Acronis and my blood turned to ice. I remembered the person lying on the ground. The three men surrounding me. My heartbeat picked up speed.

I must have gotten the lump when I'd hit the ground.

They'd said their boss wanted to see me, but didn't say where he was. If two of them weren't Shakiran, it made sense that I would be taken off-world, but to where?

If they knew about Althar 3, maybe they were from Althar or a neighbouring planet, but could be from any planet between there and Shakira.

I struggled to slow my breathing as my heart continued to race.

Although my legs didn't feel like they could support me, I shuffled to the door and pressed my thumb to the lock. It didn't respond and my stomach dropped. Locked in again.

My fists clenched. How was I going to cope with being locked in a small room for who knew how long?

I pounded on the door. "Hey! Let me out of here!"

I looked around for any cameras in the room and couldn't see anything obvious, so I pounded on the door again. After some more pounding and yelling, the door swished open and a man with orange eyes stood in the hall.

I moved forward and threw a punch at his face, which he blocked easily. "Calm down, Shakiran. We're not here to hurt you."

Whatever they'd drugged me with was still making me sluggish.

"I don't believe you. You kidnapped me."

He relaxed his stance as he looked me up and down. "Boss's orders. I told you. Nothin' personal."

Another man appeared in the doorway with the same creepy orange eyes. Their pupils were vertical slits. I'd only ever seen eyes like that on reptiles. Other than that, they looked more-or-less like humans with overly-large mouths.

The new arrival smiled. "Hello, sleepyhead."

I narrowed my eyes. "Who are you and where are you taking me?"

His smile widened. "We told you. To our boss."

I clenched my jaw. "That doesn't tell me anything. Where is your boss?"

"Not on Shakira."

I clenched my fists. He noticed. "Don't talk in circles."

His face was devoid of expression. "The planet, Korovska."

I'd never heard of it. "Where's that?"

"Far awa—"

"I'm warning you."

"Far away on the Fringe." He smirked and fingered a device on his belt that looked like a kind of stunner.

"*What?*"

The smirk turned to a sneer. "Are you deaf?"

"I can't go all the way out there. It'll take two weeks to get there. I can't be gone for four weeks. I have things to do."

I wasn't about to tell them my plans. That someone was going to be looking at the house. That I would be looking at a new house in a town that was far enough away from my home town that I wouldn't have a reason to be visiting any of the memory-filled places from my childhood.

He chuckled. "Korovska has better ships. It will not take us that long to get there. We are about quarter of the way already."

"How long have I been out?"

"All night and all day."

My stomach sank. No wonder I felt so terrible. And although my stomach was queasy, I was actually hungry.

"How long does it take to get there?"

"About six standard days."

That was still too long for me to be away. I gritted my teeth. "So what happens now?"

Did I have to spend the next five days on this ship with these aliens with sinister-looking eyes?

"We feed you and give you a place to sleep so we can deliver you alive. We take you to our boss. We get paid."

I sucked in a breath. Despite the overly-simplified answer, I was relieved that they would 'deliver' me alive. Then a voice in my head reminded me that they'd basically said that from the beginning.

I didn't trust these people, but I couldn't go six days without food. "What's for dinner, then?"

It turned out dinner was heated ration packs from a food dispenser. They were hot, but lacked flavour. The only drinks available were water and alcohol. They gave me water.

"So, what happened to the Shakiran?" I asked after I'd eaten.

"He did his job. Got paid. No need to bring him along. We got what we wanted."

I bristled at the idea of a fellow Shakiran helping these aliens kidnap me for money, but I knew that being from my home planet didn't automatically make him a decent person.

I knew I didn't have a choice at this point; I had to put up with them for the rest of this trip, give their boss what he wanted, then endure the trip home. I'd still be gone too long. My plans were ruined.

The woman I'd paid to check in on the plants for me while I'd gone to Althar 3 was no longer needed when I'd come back home again. I hoped the watering system would be able to keep them all alive while I was gone this time. I needed to contact the agent to tell them I wasn't able to make it to the appointment for me to look at the new house or be present while people inspected the old one. I could definitely kiss both of those sales goodbye.

"Can I at least get a message to someone to tell them where I am?"

They both laughed. Loudly. For a long time.

CHAPTER 24
Welcome to Dekora Corporation

The rest of the journey wasn't a pleasant experience. Sharing a small ship with two creepy-eyed aliens who'd kidnapped me for money and who were armed with stunners had me stressed and anxious. Five days is a long time to be on edge and constantly on your guard. I'd hardly slept.

The opportunity to overpower them never presented itself, which was frustrating.

If they'd made any *ungentlemanly* advances, I would've defended myself without hesitation, despite my agreement to give their boss what he wanted so I could go home, and my reluctance to hurt anyone. There was a line and I would not let them cross it.

After a surprisingly smooth landing, we were met by two men in black uniforms wearing stunners and laser pistols on their belts and I was taken to see the 'boss.' Their orange eyes confirmed they were the same race as my kidnappers.

We arrived at a door made of an unusual metal with a sign across it written in an oddly-shaped text. The office was spacious with a large desk in the centre. The boss was a large man with the same sinister eyes and big mouth as the others and his malicious smile sent a shiver down my spine.

He looked up at me and raised his eyebrows. "My, Shakirans *are* tall, aren't they?"

His voice was a deep baritone and he rested his hands on his substantial stomach.

One of the guards guided me to a seat by holding my elbow and I resisted the urge to pull away from him.

I sat on the edge of the seat with my back ramrod-straight. "What do you want?"

"I am Lundahl Saizen and you are here to help the Dekora Corporation."

"Why kidnap me? Why not ask me what I know? You can't just go around stealing people from their home planets and dragging them across the universe."

He looked bored. "According to whom?"

"According to Intergalactic Law."

He sniffed. "No imbecile in a suit or robe will tell us what we can and cannot do. I have waited a long time to see this research come to fruition. We will get what we need from you. One way or another."

I suppressed a shudder. "So, what do you want? I don't know anything about the technical side of what they did to me."

"That is not a problem. We have that information."

I scowled. "*What?* So you don't need me. Why drag me all the way out here? What do you want with me?"

"You only need to know that you will be kept alive. You will further our studies. You will help us succeed."

"Succeed in what?"

He looked at the guards. "Take her away."

My mouth fell open. "They said I had to talk to you and help you with your research. I'm here to help you and you're sending me out the door?"

He didn't even look at me. "Take her to Madhur."

One of them grabbed my arm and 'guided' me out of my seat. "Let's go."

I was led down a hallway or two where we came to another metal door. My kidnappers had disappeared. I clenched my fists. Probably gone to get paid.

We entered the room. This wasn't an office. It looked more like something out of a horror HoloMovie with two beds with straps fitted across them and sinister-looking implements on trays. Possibly the scariest thing in the room was the orange-eyed man with the reddish-brown hair.

"Ah, welcome to Dekora Corporation. I am Doctor Jozean Madhur." He wasn't smiling and his greeting was anything but welcoming. "You are here to help us. I will start with the basics."

I cringed. What were 'the basics'?

He waved a hand toward the nearest bed. "Sit."

I stared at those straps and my feet were stuck to the floor.

"I said, SIT!"

That got my legs moving and I perched myself on the edge of the bed.

Madhur started by taking my blood pressure, then my temperature. He took some blood, tested my reflexes, and tested my hearing and eyesight. He also recorded my height and weight.

The two guards stood at the doorway looking bored. I wondered if all Korovskans had orange eyes or whether there were different colours.

As I waited impatiently for him to finish, I noticed there were marks here and there on the walls, like someone had thrown things around in here.

My concentration was broken by Madhur telling me to lie down so he could take my blood pressure again. As I lowered myself to the mattress, a shiver raced up my spine.

My feet hung over the edge of the bed. I was too tall.

He left me there for a minute or two, then took my blood pressure.

I wondered what sort of tests were next.

"Okay. Roll over so you're facing away from me."

"Why?"

He sighed heavily. "Don't ask dumb questions and keep still."

My blood ran cold. "What are you going to do?"

"I'm going to remove your tracker."

"*What?* What tracker?"

"Starrick implanted trackers into all of his specimens back at Maztec. Yours has to be removed."

"Removed?" My stomach sank. "Is it faulty?"

"No."

"Then why?"

"Roll over now, or we'll make you do it."

Panic rose and it became harder to breathe. "I can't. I don't know what you're going to do to me."

"Guards."

They didn't hesitate and simply rolled me over despite my struggles, holding me in place. They were too strong.

I heard the sound of wheels on the hard floor. The jostle of metallic objects.

My hair was moved out the way and a cold Injectorgun pressed against the back of my neck. My heart pounded faster and I couldn't slow my breathing.

The area was soon numb and the pushing sensation told me he was cutting my flesh. My stomach roiled and I wanted to scream. And throw up. I scrunched up my toes and clenched my fists.

"Keep still!"

"I can't."

"You will if you don't want me to cause some serious damage."

Chapter 25

You Will Need to Be Trained

I froze. He was right. How close was he to my spine? I forced myself to keep so still that my muscles began to ache.

More pushing. Nothing. Then a strange vibration for several seconds, which was probably him closing up the wound.

"You can release her now."

I relaxed a bit, but didn't make a move to get up or turn over. I didn't want to see the blood.

There was a slim chance Jannali might have been able to find me using the tracker, but it was probably too small for its signal to reach another planet.

Why hadn't they told me I had a tracker under my skin? Maybe they didn't know.

Maybe they'd used it to track me down on Shakira.

Wait. That was how Starrick had found Tamisan in the middle of a dense jungle with no air support to aid him.

"Right. Lie on your back."

I sucked in a breath, wondering what he would do next.

"I won't say it again."

I rolled over to find him standing over me with a wiring harness in his long fingers.

He jiggled it in front of me. "I'm going to put this on your head and monitor your brainwaves."

I let him put it on, relieved he wasn't going to cut me again.

I tried not to squirm while he watched the screens and made notes on a Palm-pad. I resisted the urge to shut everything out by closing my eyes. I needed to know where he was at every second.

He turned to me and I managed to not cringe. "Now we test your abilities. What is your T-Rating?"

"I have not been Rated yet," I told him.

His bushy eyebrows rose.

I wasn't about to tell him I was a T1. It would be better if he thought I was useless, not the strongest Talent possible. If I wasn't valuable, they might send me home sooner.

"I have only had some basic training. It's not easy to have Talent thrown at you suddenly when you're not prepared for it."

The eyebrows slammed back down. "Are you saying that you don't know how to use your abilities?"

"No, not quite. I mean, I can do some stuff, but not much."

He pinched the bridge of his nose and I found myself enjoying the expressions playing out across his face as I spoke. I had to stop talking before I overdid it and made him really angry.

"What *can* you do?"

"I can have a telepathic conversation and I can lift a few small objects. That's about it."

I had worked on my control these last couple of weeks and I'd improved, but I wouldn't tell him that.

He took a deep breath and let it out slowly. I managed to not laugh.

"Okay. Do it."

Which one first? "Is there someone I can have a telepathic conversation with?"

"No. Lift something."

I looked around for something to lift and saw the blood-covered tracker on a nearby tray. I tried not to think about it while I looked for something small and clean and preferably unbreakable.

He held out a hand with a plastic cup resting on his palm. "Lift this."

I tried to calm my nerves by taking a deep breath and did my best to ignore his glare.

I managed to lift it up, let it hover for a while, then set it back down. I would not do anything more complex in front of this man.

He pinched the bridge of his nose again. "You will need to be trained."

"What for? You only wanted me to help you with your research, not stay here and continue the training I can do at home on Shakira."

He took the cup away and mumbled under his breath, turning to his screens.

After what seemed like hours, but was probably about five minutes, he took the harness off and said, "Get her out of my sight."

I may have been rudely ejected from that awful room, but I was so glad to be out of there.

I was taken to a cafeteria but the food was unrecognisable. The girl behind the counter looked to be about fourteen with her long black hair tied into plaits and her tear-smudged eye makeup. She served up a few dishes of some mushy-looking food and passed me a drink as she attempted a conversation. I wasn't in the mood to talk.

I thanked her and sat at a nearby table. I was the only person in here and I guessed that they'd planned it that way so they could limit my contact with people.

I had no idea what I was eating, but two out of the three dishes tasted okay. Better than ration packs. The third dish was so bitter that it took several mouthfuls of the other food and some of the drink — which turned out to be water — to get rid of the taste.

They let me take my time eating, so I hoped that meant Madhur didn't want me back in there anytime soon.

That was fine with me.

I was lost in thought when the girl approached me. "Can I sit with you?"

I looked at her bloodshot eyes and red nose and nodded.

"Thank you. I just..." She looked down into her lap.

"It's okay. What's up?"

I had no idea why I wanted to help her, but she looked so distraught, I couldn't help it.

"I... just need someone to talk to is all." She sniffed. "I'm just feeling down." She made a move to get up. "I shouldn't be bothering you. Sorry..."

"No. It's okay."

Maybe I was desperate for someone to talk to as well.

She sniffed again. "Do you know much about how to deal with boys? Sorry. That was a dumb question. I mean, I have a partner — Neiko — and we've been together since I was eighteen, but... but I think he's gonna leave me."

I was the last person in the universe to be asking about this stuff. "I don't know how much help I'll be, but what makes you think that?"

"He says that I'm distant, you know? That I don't tell him stuff. I don't let him close."

"Do you think you do that?"

"I don't know. I guess. I have trouble, see. I had a bad relationship before. I got hurt bad. I can't... I can't tell him what's in my heart. I'm scared."

"He knows about the other relationship, yes?"

"No. I'm scared to tell him."

"You need to—"

"Time to go."

CHAPTER 26
Could I Ever Be Happy?

I turned. The guards were standing over us. The girl stood and scurried away.

I called after her. "What's your name?"

"Arietta."

She turned and slipped through the staff entrance.

I stood and looked down at the guards. "We were in the middle of a conversation."

The taller one smirked. "We have our orders."

My stomach sank at the thought of going back into that room with Madhur, but I followed them anyway. What else could I do?

I needn't have worried. They took me to a small room with an adjoining bathroom and the door swished closed behind me.

Relief flooded through me, but I knew I couldn't relax completely.

I tried the door and as expected, it was locked.

I used the bathroom and saw that they'd put out clothes for me to wear. Dark grey cargo pants and a slightly lighter grey top. The sleeves and the pant legs were a bit short and I was reminded of being stuck at Maztec. This was chillingly similar and I sucked in a breath. This one was going to be a lot harder to get out of if they didn't let me go home like they'd promised.

Only, they hadn't promised.

As far as I was concerned, their word meant nothing. These people had no honour. They were the kind of people who got what they wanted and didn't care how they got it.

I was in deep trouble.

I sat on the edge of the bed. I had no idea how I could possibly escape, but my mind kept ticking over, trying to find something.

Arietta kept intruding on those thoughts. Why had she chosen me to pour her heart out to? Maybe because I was the only female around.

But she'd chosen the wrong person to ask. I had no idea when it came to anything regarding relationships. You couldn't call what Yuriko and I had at the university a relationship when I'd run out on him the moment he'd kissed me.

You couldn't call what happened between Janssen and I a relationship either. We were friends. That was all.

He'd tried to take things further and I'd run out on him too. I could see the pattern. I knew I'd hurt both of them, but I was scared. I didn't want to get hurt. I'd lost so much in my life. My chest ached thinking about it.

My mind drew parallels between my situation and Arietta's, both afraid to let someone in, but it only reinforced the fact that I needed to start building the walls around my heart again. I needed to build them up like the wall in my mind — my mental shield.

That was a good analogy. Something to focus on.

I started by pushing all the pain in my chest down into a small space and locking it away. Again. I lay down on the bed and concentrated on getting rid of my heartache.

⸻ ◆ ⸻

I wasn't sure how long I'd been in the room for and maybe I'd fallen asleep at some point, but I was starting to feel quite hungry when the door opened and made me jump. The same two guards were standing there as if they hadn't moved.

The taller one stepped forward. "We will take you to have your evening meal."

I gave a curt nod and followed them, glad I would be able to eat again and wondering if Arietta would still be there.

I honestly hoped she wasn't. It had taken a long time to calm my mind and get my emotions under control. It should have been easy; I'd been doing it all my life. But lately it had been so much harder to do.

As soon as we entered the cafeteria, my chest tightened.

Although her eyes glistened with unshed tears, Arietta beamed at me. "Hi! I'm glad you're back. What would you like this time?"

I pointed at the horrible food I'd had before. "Not that one. It was awful. Too bitter." I pointed at the other two. "They weren't so bad."

She kept the smile in place. "Okay. I'll give you something else to try."

She gave me the two I'd had before, plus a couple of new ones that looked just as unappetising.

One of the new ones was nice and the other was actually delicious. I surprised myself. I'd expected something quite different. I hoped my stomach didn't have a bad reaction to the foreign food.

As I expected, Arietta came to sit with me before I'd even finished. I tried to mentally prepare myself so I wouldn't feel as dreadful as I had before.

It didn't take her long to get straight back to our conversation. "Thanks for listening to me before."

"That's okay."

"You see, me and Neiko have been real happy together. We have so much in common, you know." She looked at the guards and lowered her voice. "When he kisses me, I feel truly loved. You know how that feels?"

The memory of Janssen's kisses sprang into my mind and all the emotions and sensations flooded through me. Yes, I knew how it felt. The feeling of melting on the spot. The fire in his touch. The longing I didn't know I'd been feeling finally being fulfilled.

I nodded. I couldn't speak.

"He's my everything. We've been together since I was eighteen and he was twenty. He's all I ever wanted."

My vision blurred.

She looked at me with such hope and I somehow managed to get some words out. "He feels the same way about you, yes?"

"Oh, yes. He tells me all the time. He don't have trouble talking about it. That's all me."

I took a mouthful of goop, didn't have to chew it, and swallowed. "So what made him say he's going to leave?"

"Neiko wants to move in together and that's when I panicked. I... I can't do that. I want to... but I can't."

"Why not? What about this other relationship you told me about? What happened?"

She looked down in her lap. "We were together for a couple of years and when we was seventeen, we moved in together —

that's totally allowed in our culture. But then as soon as we got a place together, he changed. He was so possessive and acted like he owned me. He started hitting me, only soft at first, but then it got harder and I knew he weren't playing like he said he was. It took a long time and a huge black eye for me to get out."

Tears ran down her cheeks and she sniffed.

I wasn't sure what to say. "You did the right thing, getting away from him."

"But now Neiko messaged me in my break and said he thinks we should break up because I won't answer him about getting a place together and he says I'm not really talking to him anymore. I never have, really. I don't know what to do. I'm pregnant. I don't wanna lose him. I can't lose him. Not now. I don't wanna face bringing up a baby on my own."

What could I say? My heart was breaking for her. She had to do something, and fast.

My face itched and when I scratched it, my cheek was wet. Why was I crying?

She took a deep breath. "I was gonna tell him about the other relationship, like you said, but I couldn't do it. My fingers wouldn't type the words."

I was surprised she'd want to have such an important conversation in text messages.

"It's not something you should try to explain in a text-only message. You need to be talking to him face-to-face — not even a Vid call. It won't be easy, but just force yourself to do it. This is too important for you to give in to your fears. He needs to know why you are scared and why you keep shutting him out. And you need to somehow tear down the wall you've built around your heart and let him in. Honesty is the only way to really make a relationship work. It's the only way you can be truly happy."

Where was all this coming from?

I had no idea, but it had poured out of my mouth like a river. And the scariest thing was, I think I was talking more to myself than to Arietta. Telling myself to talk to Janssen. To tell him how I felt. Then I'd be truly happy. But would I?

Could I ever be happy?

CHAPTER 27
Battle-Ready

The following morning, I was taken to the same lab and the wiring harness was back on my head. They'd ignored my questions about when I could go home.

I sat there silently, feeling strange with my feet hanging over the edge of the bed and trying to keep my mind occupied with something other than Janssen and my conversation with Arietta. Every time Madhur walked past the foot of the bed, I thought he'd bump into my feet.

It was hard not to think about what he was doing and why they wanted me here. My mind conjured up too many awful scenarios. I needed a distraction. Surely they could have music playing or a screen on the ceiling, but maybe that was part of the test. Maybe I wasn't supposed to be doing much or thinking too much.

I wondered if I could mess up their results by reciting all the plant names I could think of. But that reminded me of spending time with Janssen in the hydroponics garden. There was a tightness in my chest.

My heart and my head were a jumbled mess after talking to Arietta. After the advice I'd given that had come from somewhere inside me. I'd lain awake for hours wrestling with my wild emotions and conflicting thoughts. I'd been wrong about Janssen. Wrong about a lot of things.

I had to think. I had to sort my head out — and my heart. I had strong feelings for him. I knew now that if I wanted to be happy, I needed to be honest with myself and honest with Janssen about how I felt.

But what if they never found him?

The pain of losing him; it was there, waiting in the wings. Waiting for me to find out he's gone forever. Then it would pounce and I'd be lost.

I relived the moment he kissed me. My lips tingled with the memory. The way his lips felt; warm and soft. His hands in my hair. His hands touching me, cupping my cheek. The look in his eyes.

I'd never had that before. Never felt that way. The realization that life is meaningless without love had probably come too late. I'd spent my whole life running from it and only managed to make myself miserable.

I had to pull my thoughts away from that. I had to keep it together. I had to find a way out of here. I wondered if I could somehow get Arietta to help me. Maybe she could…

I didn't know what I could get her to do, even if she was willing to help. The guards would be there watching.

My heart sank a little.

I'd been told as soon as I'd entered the room that they'd assigned a trainer from Taon to teach me how to use my Talent. There was a sense of deja vu and I wanted to run through the halls till I couldn't run any further.

Not another trainer. Was that four already?

The fact that the trainer was from Taon probably meant these Korovskans didn't have Talent, or that it was rare here.

All the pieces fell into place. They had all the information from Starrick. They'd put this harness on my head twice now. That was how Starrick had transferred Zhenna's consciousness into the native's body. That was how he'd transferred her Talent to me.

I sat up so suddenly that Madhur jumped backwards.

"What are you doing?" he squeaked. Then he cleared his throat. "You need to keep still."

I glared at him. "What are you doing to me?"

"You are helping us with research."

"No. What are you *really* doing?" I pulled the harness off my head and he protested loudly. I waved the wires at him. "Starrick used this equipment to transfer the Talent to my brain. So what are *you* doing with it?"

"Stop this right now! I don't need to tell you anything."

I stood and looked down at him and I could feel my Talent there inside me, waiting to be released. "Tell me!"

He held his ground. "You're not in a position to demand anything, but I will tell you anyway. We brought you here to use your Talent to improve our species." My chest tightened. "We have since found the source of your Talent." *Tamisan?* "We will use whichever mind is viable."

"Tamisan is here?"

"Yes. She will be used, then trained. You have previous training, so you will be ready sooner."

"What are you talking about? Tamisan has better control over her Talent. She has the memories of the Althari woman to fall back on. I have nothing."

"I am not referring to Talent training. Military training. You Shakirans are taught to fight, yes? You will both be made battle-ready as quickly as possible." My head spun. "We will create an army of perfect soldiers who can read minds, communicate silently, move things kinetically, and teleport to their destinations with ease." Nausea rose in my stomach. "We will be unstoppable."

CHAPTER 28
We Will Be Victorious

My head was going to explode. "NO! You can't do that! You will have an unfair advantage in war. Other armies will have no chance."

"That is the general idea. Centuries of research and experimentation will come to fruition. We will be victorious."

I could hardly breathe. "No."

I couldn't believe it. They were serious. They were going to use Tamisan's Talent to create an unstoppable army. So many people would die. The thought of all those families living through the hell I'd been through tore at my insides. I'd tried to devote my life to healing and preventing death and the heartache I carried with me every day, and they were going to use me to kill. To give them an unfair advantage in every battle.

It hit me hard. The pain that crushed me when the men at the door told us Mother and Father weren't ever coming home. The sound of Gran's sobs when she'd lost the love of her life. The way I couldn't breathe properly when I'd learned Eli had been shot down over Valora.

The tears came then. I couldn't stop them. My heart hadn't hardened. I'd only tucked the pain away in a corner, and it had been waiting for the right time to tear me apart.

I couldn't do it. I couldn't stand by and let them do this. How many lives would be lost? How far would they take this war? It could spread from this galaxy and into the next. With Talent as rare as it is on Shakira, they'd walk right over us.

These people were crazy and were determined to see it through.

My face was hot and my palms hurt as my fingernails dug in. Madhur had taken a step back; maybe he saw something in my eyes.

A few things flew off the shelves and shattered on the floor. The guards reached for their pistols.

Madhur glanced back. "Do *not* use your pistols!"

As their hands moved from the pistols to their stunners, the energy inside me burst from my outstretched hands and all three of them flew backwards into the walls and slid down into crumpled piles of arms and legs. More equipment fell over and things clattered to the floor.

Before I knew what I was doing, I was running down hallways, looking for a way out. I had to get out of here. I couldn't stand it any longer.

Was there a way to somehow stop them from doing this?

Maybe I could find Tamisan and we could escape together.

I looked more closely at the doors I passed. Was she behind one of them? How could I tell? Would they open for me? If they did, would I be faced with more armed guards?

I kept going, my direction aimless, my hopes dwindling.

I rounded a corner and someone shouted for me to stop, but I flung my energy outwards, knocking over the six or seven people that had taken up positions in the corridor.

They all went down, but I couldn't stop to think about it, I had to keep going.

A few more turns and I thought I could hear voices and footsteps behind me somewhere.

At the next corner, I found myself face-to-face with little Arietta.

Her face lit up. "Larissa! I did it! I took your advice. I went to see Neiko and we had a real good talk."

Someone was coming. I could hear footsteps approaching. "That's great, but I gotta go."

I started down another hallway.

She frowned. "But I gotta tell ya. We sorted stuff out. We're good now. We're gonna find a place and—"

Searing pain sliced through me and as my muscles locked up and I fell to the floor, Arietta screamed.

I knew what was coming. The blackness of unconsciousness. But it didn't come. I writhed around on the floor with no control over my body while Arietta cried and apologized and yelled at the person holding the stunner.

Intense heat radiated through me and I was on fire. I had no idea how long it lasted, but once it stopped, the relief was blissful.

My muscles went limp and I couldn't move. A sea of faces appeared above me; Arietta had been replaced by Madhur. I couldn't hear what he was saying, but I could see his sneer.

I had the sense of movement and assumed I was being carried. I couldn't feel my body. Then the blackness finally took me.

—◆—

I woke with a start. My eyes were full of sand and every muscle screamed at me. What happened? Why did I feel this way?

My mind seemed to wade through mud until the memories flooded in. Finding out what they planned to do with my Talent. Hurting people as they tried to stop me. Searching for Tamisan and trying to escape. Arietta distracting me. The stunner blast that lasted so much longer than it should have...

What modifications had they made to it? A stunner blast usually made someone lose consciousness after a few seconds. That thing was a torture device.

Is that what they'd resorted to?

They probably didn't care in the slightest. Torture would be way down on the list of despicable things they were willing to do.

I thought about Starrick testing me to make sure the stunner blast didn't do any damage and cringed. The Korovskans must have modified it so it didn't do any permanent damage, otherwise they wouldn't have risked using it on me. I was too valuable to them.

I recognised the room I'd been in before. Someone had put me back into the bed. My head pounded and movement was difficult, so of course my bladder let me know right then that it needed to be emptied.

I moaned. How long had I been out?

I tried to hold out a bit longer to let my muscles recover first, but I couldn't do it. I had to get up.

I rolled over toward the edge of the bed and flopped onto the floor. Raising myself up onto my hands and knees was painful and humiliating, even though I was alone, but it was nothing compared to crawling to the bathroom and doing what I needed to do without being able to stand.

When I was almost back to the bed, I decided that climbing back up there was too hard and resolved to lie on the floor, but after about a minute, I had to move. The floor was too cold and too hard on my aching muscles.

After dragging myself up onto the bed again, the tears started. How could I get out of here? How could I stop them?

There was no way to stop them now. They'd probably taken all they needed from my brain before I ripped the harness off — and they had Tamisan. I didn't know enough about computers or how they could even transfer brainwaves from one person to another, so I had no idea how to stop them from replicating the process.

Was the information somehow stored on the computer? That made sense because there wasn't someone next to me wearing a wiring harness. And Tamisan wasn't in the room when they transferred her Talent to me.

My head hurt trying to figure it out. My head hurt anyway.

I wasn't sure how long I lay there in the darkness — a few hours maybe. I was glad no one had come in and demanded I get up. If they wanted me to go back to the lab, they would have to carry me. I cringed at the thought.

The spot on the back of my neck where they'd removed the tracker was sore again. That was odd. It had begun to heal, so why was it hurting? Maybe it had something to do with the extended stunner blast.

I thought about what I'd done when I'd run. All of the guards I'd blasted with my Talent. I'd hit them pretty hard, especially the ones in the halls. One in particular had hit a wall and crumpled to the floor in an awkward position. Was he dead? Did he break his neck in the fall? Had I caused another death?

It was something I didn't want to think about, but found myself dwelling on it anyway. At the very least, some of those people needed medical attention.

It had happened again. I'd been taken against my will and forced into a situation where I'd had to defend myself and people had gotten hurt or killed.

I sighed heavily. I'd spent my whole life trying to avoid violence of any kind. My face was hot and I tried to clench my fists, but my muscles were jelly.

These people needed to be held accountable for all the things they'd done, but also needed to be stopped before they succeeded with their plans.

Nausea rose as my imagination painted the picture. Thousands of people with the same abilities as me who didn't know how to use them or control them. Then going through training and being sent out to fight. Winning battle after battle, killing thousands — maybe even millions — of people. All of the families and friends of those people feeling the deep grief that I dealt with every day of my life.

The magnitude of it had me struggling to breathe. So many needless deaths. So much destruction.

My head spun. There was no way to stop it. Even if I refused to help them and they killed me, they still had Tamisan.

Tears flooded my eyes and I sobbed. For all those families. For Tamisan. For me.

A long time later, I finally stopped and my breathing slowed.

One thing I did know; I would *not* help them. It was probably too late and they probably had everything they needed, but I didn't care if they killed me — I was *not* going to cooperate any further.

CHAPTER 29

I Was in So Much Trouble

I had no idea how much time had passed before the door swished open and light flooded in from the hall.

I squinted in the harsh light and could make out one of the guards carrying a tray of food over to the small table in the corner. I expected him to turn around and leave, but he stopped and looked down at me.

"You had to be punished, but you will be allowed to eat. Your tracker has been reinserted. It has been modified so it blocks your Talent. You will not try to escape again or your punishment will be severe."

And with that, he spun on his heel and strode out. The door slid shut and I was left in the dark, speechless.

They'd somehow modified the tracker to block my Talent? How could they do that?

It didn't matter how. I dragged myself up and switched on the light. I concentrated on a fork sitting on the side of the food tray and tried to lift it.

Nothing.

I tried again.

Nothing.

I should have been able to do something that simple, even in my current state.

I let down the mental wall in my mind and heard nothing. They weren't lying. My Talent was gone.

I was in so much trouble.

———◆———

After spending what seemed like an eternity lying in bed, I'd forced myself to get up and get moving. I had to be able to defend myself. I'd started with gentle stretching and switched to doing some slow movements, then eventually moved on to some exercises.

Judging by how many meals they'd delivered, I guessed that it was the following evening. Once I'd had my evening meal and done some gentle exercises, I left the bedside lamp on and headed into the bathroom. I couldn't stop the thoughts swirling in my mind and washed my face to try to clear my head. I tried to push thoughts of an unstoppable army away, with no success.

I turned the light off and as I headed back into my room, a man appeared in front of me out of nowhere. I instinctively crouched low and took his legs out from under him.

He hit the floor with a grunt, then leapt to his feet and assumed a fighting stance, but I was ready to defend myself if needed. "What do you want?"

"Hey! Shh. Take it easy. I'm not here to hurt you." His voice was almost a whisper.

"Where did you—" I sucked in a breath. "Braydac? What are you doing here?"

His eyebrows rose. "Larissa?"

"Yes. I don't understand. How did you get here?"

He pointed to a spot over his shoulder and spoke directly into my mind. *"There's a camera in this room, but not in your bathroom. Can we go in there to talk?"*

I indicated he should go first. I followed him in and he gestured for me to close the door. I debated whether to do as he'd said, but if there was a camera in the corner of the main room, we were still visible.

I closed the door, but remained on my guard. I wished I could use my Talent to speak to him telepathically. "Start talking."

"The Korovska spoke of you, but I didn't know you were actually here. *Dammit.* This changes everything."

I clenched my fists. "You haven't answered my question. What are you doing here?"

He relaxed his stance. "I'm here with Tamisan."

I gasped. "Is she alright?"

"Yes. For the moment."

"But what are you doing in my room?"

"I was looking around the base. Finding you was an accident." I relaxed a bit, but wasn't about to trust him. "It wasn't part of my plan, but we need to get you out of here now. Before they... how much do you know about what they're doing here?"

"How are you going to get me out of here? We're on a planet called Korovska."

"I can teleport you and Tamisan out of here. Tell me what you know."

I sighed. "They are trying to create an army of Talents, starting with me and Tamisan."

He grimaced. "Yep. They've already started. Our plan is to destroy their data and get the fuck out of here."

"How?"

"I found something to do the job. Don't worry about that."
He stepped closer. "Do you wanna get out of here?"

"Of course I do. But I tried to run and when they tried to stop me, I hurt some people. Badly. And then they punished me."

"We've been on the receiving end of their punishments too. It's not gonna stop us though."

"I don't want to hurt anyone else."

"Oh, boohoo. Wake up. They aren't gonna play nice. They're creating an army of unstoppable Talents. They're gonna kill millions. Billions. They aren't gonna let you walk out of here. None of us will get out of here alive if we don't go now. Do you want to get out of here or not?"

"Yes."

"Okay. Here's what you're gonna do. Go to bed and shut off the light like usual and I'll come get you in the dark."

"That's it?"

"I'll port you out of this room. Then we'll blow up their computers and be outta here."

He made it sound so simple. Too simple.

"But—"

"Oh, I'll disable the Talent blocker in your tracker too. Will you be able to defend yourself?"

How did he know about the tracker? Probably because Tamisan had one too. "Maybe. I'm not that good yet. But I'm Shakiran. I can fight."

"Okay. That'll have to do. Be ready. I'll be back soon. I have to get Tamisan first."

I had a million questions. "But—"

"I don't have time to answer questions. We need to get out of here and tonight is the night. Will you be ready?"

"I— Yes. I'll be waiting for you."

And with that, he disappeared.

It was like a whirlwind had blown in here, knocked everything onto the floor, and left. My mind reeled. Did I dare to
hope that I could get out of here?

It was surreal, but I had to make sure I was in position when
he came back — *if* he came back — so I used the bathroom and
climbed into bed as if nothing had changed, leaving my shoes
on. I hoped no one saw Braydac appear in my room.

Once the light was off, my brain was flooded with doubts.
What if he didn't come back? What if someone saw him on
camera? What if the camera could pick up our conversation,
even through the closed door? What if something went wrong
and we didn't make it out of here? What would be my punishment?

I had to stop myself. Those thoughts weren't helpful.

I tried to relax and slow my breathing. Waiting was hard. I
was amped up and ready to run, but had to lie still, not knowing
exactly what we were about to do or when he'd come back.

I thought about what he'd said about being able to defend
myself. Of course I could — especially when it came to combat
without using my Talent. But I'd spent my whole life running
from that part of myself. Not wanting to use the skills I'd learned
when I was younger. My mind kept circling back to those people
I'd hurt and the dead guy at Maztec.

But then something kind of clicked in place in my brain. Yes,
fighting was wrong. War was wrong. But the universe wasn't
all sunshine and rainbows. Starrick and the people in this place
were proof of that. There were too many people in the universe
who were out to kill or hurt you or take what wasn't theirs, and
that meant no matter how much you wanted it to be otherwise,
at times like these, you had to step up and defend yourself and

do what's right. To stop them from causing harm. And we *had* to stop them from causing harm.

Maybe if I'd realized that sooner, I might have been able to avoid being dragged here in the first place. I might have been able to prevent us being captured by Starrick's men. Things could have been different.

But there was no use in lamenting the past. I had to look to the present and the immediate future. When Braydac returned, I would not stand by and let them rescue me. I would be an active participant in this escape.

I tossed and turned and couldn't settle. The waiting was getting to me.

Then I heard a noise beside the bed and Braydac's voice in my mind. *"Larissa. It's me, Braydac. Slide out of bed so you're crouching on the floor, then grab my hand."*

As soon as I hit the floor, Braydac's hand found mine and we teleported to what looked like a storeroom. I squinted in the sudden light as we both stood up. Dizziness that had me pitching forward, but kept my feet. Tamisan stepped forward with a huge smile on her face and my heart leapt.

I wrapped my arms around her. *"Tamisan! It's so good to see you!"*

CHAPTER 30

I Don't Need Him

I was surprised I could use my Talent; Braydac had kept his word about disabling the Talent blocker.

Her arms came up around me and Braydac said, *"We don't have time for happy reunions. We need to get moving."*

I somehow knew he'd sent that thought to both of us.

"Yes. We can have a three-way conversation by sending the thoughts out to two people," he said.

That would make this operation a lot easier.

He grabbed a couple of backpacks from a cupboard with a broken door in the corner of the room and held one out to Tamisan. *"Here. Put this on."*

She hesitated. *"What's in it?"*

"Explosives."

She grimaced. *"Okay."*

His eyebrows drew together. *"What's wrong?"*

"Now I have to make sure I don't blow myself up."

He rolled his eyes. *"There's not much chance of that. They aren't really that dangerous without their trigger."*

"Oh."

He gave Tamisan a stunner. *"Take this. It's set to stun."* She took it and he pulled another one from his pack for himself. *"Sorry, Larissa. I didn't have time to get one for you."*

I nodded. That was fair enough. I was a last-minute addition to their plans.

I cringed as I noticed Tamisan was pointing her stunner directly at Braydac and he carefully pushed her hand down.

Her eyebrows rose, then she let out a breath. *"Don't worry. I won't shoot you. I'd never get out of here if I did that."*

He smiled.

She turned to me and held the stunner out — handle first. *"Here. Take it. You'll need it more than me."*

I smiled. *"Thank you."*

I was more confident now that I had a weapon as I was more skilled with a stunner or pistol than with my Talent.

Braydac took a deep breath. *"We need to stick together in case something goes wrong and I have to port us out of the base completely."*

We nodded.

He took our hands and we were suddenly in a huge room full of computer terminals and what looked like lots of cupboards. It must have been the mainframe.

The dizziness wasn't as severe this time.

He pulled some small rectangular devices from his backpack and handed them to us. *"Put these near the storage drives and press the green button once they're in place."*

Tamisan nodded and headed over to some of the cupboards, but I wasn't sure what was what. I didn't know computers like she did. Once she pointed out the storage drives, I quickly placed the explosives and pressed their buttons.

The second we finished, Braydac teleported us to a similar room that probably held some kind of back-ups of the data.

He turned to Tamisan. *"I've been watching the patrols. We only have ten minutes before the guards come down this way, so let's make it quick."*

They pulled the explosives from Tamisan's backpack and we wasted no time putting them in place.

Braydac pulled a black device from his backpack and told us to come to him. The door swished open and I fired my stunner as I ducked for cover. A man fell to the floor, convulsing as he went, and I was pleased with my accuracy after such a long time without any weapons practice.

We weren't close enough for Braydac to touch us, so I quickly looked around the room. Tamisan was behind a desk in a corner and Braydac was crawling across the floor toward me with a laser burn to the shoulder. As he reached a hand out toward my leg, his eyes went wide and he disappeared a split second before a laser shot hit the wall. He was lucky he had good reflexes; he probably wouldn't have survived that shot.

Now Tamisan and I were stuck in the room with no way out. I didn't know Braydac, but I didn't think he'd abandon us. Maybe he would wait for the right moment to teleport back here to get us.

The first guard spoke into his Com. "Intruder alert. The Blocker has been sighted in the Backup room. Please advise."

They hadn't seen us, but it was only a matter of time.

The Com crackled and a male's voice came through. "Check the room thoroughly and report. We'll have Unit Six check his room. All available units will be put on High Alert."

"Acknowledged."

They were going to find us and we had no way out.

Someone hit the lights and a guard found Tamisan at about the same time that someone spotted me crouching in my hiding place behind a chair and desk. I swung my stunner up, but the guard had a laser pistol pointed at my head.

Then I heard the other guard say to Tamisan, "Looks like he's deserted you. He's not here to teleport you away."

I thought we were in real trouble, but Tamisan said, "I don't need him."

The room disappeared and was replaced by darkness and dizziness. I gasped.

"Larissa? Are you okay?" she asked.

"Yeah, but I can't see. Where are we?"

Something touched my arm and I flinched, but realized it was Tamisan. *"I teleported us to my room."*

"Oh. Thank you. That guard found me." I sucked in a breath. *"Do you think Braydac is okay? He got shot."*

"Braydac. Are you okay? We're back in my room. Where are you?"

His voice in my mind sounded strained. *"In that storeroom again. We can't leave yet. We need to trigger the explosions."*

I was relieved his injury hadn't caused him to pass out or teleport to the wrong place, but was also glad he was still here with us and ready to finish the job.

An alarm sounded outside.

"We need to hurry," Tamisan said as we stood up.

As the door started to open, another hand touched my arm and the room lit up with a laser blast. Before I could react, we were in the storeroom again. It took my brain a couple of seconds to process what had happened. Braydac had teleported in, grabbed us, and teleported out again.

Tamisan cried out as she rubbed her chest. "Oh!"

Braydac scowled. *"Be quiet! You'll get us killed!"*

"Sorry! I couldn't help it. I was almost hit."

"Almost *hit? How do you think* I *feel?*"

"*Oh, I'm so stupid! Sorry. Are* you *okay?*"

"*I'll live.*"

We looked at his shoulder. He would have been in an extreme amount of pain. Burns were so much worse than cuts or bruises.

Tamisan cringed. "*You need medical attention.*"

"*Yeah, later. Now I need you to focus. This trigger has a limited range. We need to be nearby when we set it off, but not close enough to cop the blast.*"

He paced the small space. "*We'll go to an office near the server room and blow the explosives, then before they know what's going on, we blow the backups. There's an office near that one too that we can use.*"

Tamisan and I exchanged a glance. Her face was pale.

"*Alright. Let's do this,*" she said.

We teleported to a dark room and I could just make out the office furniture. A digital display on the shelf behind the desk had been left on, showing photographs of a family of Korovskans in a slideshow.

Braydac pressed the trigger and a loud explosion hurt my ears, but the sound was cut off as we teleported to another dark office.

I covered my ears this time and braced myself. Braydac changed the setting on the trigger mechanism as the door to the room opened and pain burst through me, sending me into a convulsing heap on the floor. Again.

CHAPTER 31

Are We at Jannali?

When I came to, I was lying on a hard surface and bright lights hurt my eyes.

Braydac was leaning over me with a concerned look. *"Larissa? Are you okay?"*

I had trouble focusing on his face. *"Uh, yeah. I think. What happened?"*

"They stunned you and I ported you here. The fact that Tamisan hasn't followed us probably means they've stunned her too."

I tried to sit up. *"We have to go back for her."*

He gently lowered me back to the floor. *"Don't try to get up yet. We can't risk going back. We* will *get her. Just not yet. If we teleport in, they will stun us or shoot us and then no one gets to go back to Jannali."*

"But—"

"No buts. We're doing this my way." He closed his eyes for a few seconds. *"They aren't in that room anymore. She's not in her room."* Another pause. *"She's in the lab."*

My blood ran cold as my mind conjured up horrible scenarios and I tried to push them away. *"How do you know?"*

He opened his eyes. *"I can go places in my mind. Then I know if it's safe to teleport. We can't get her yet. I'm taking you back to Jannali now."*

"No! We can't just—"

But it was too late. The familiar dizziness hit me, more intense than ever this time, and we were back in a familiar-looking hallway. I heard voices and a couple of people dressed in nurses' uniforms rushed over, both talking at once as they asked who we were and where we'd come from.

All I could say was, "Are we at Jannali?"

"Yes, but where did you teleport from?"

I didn't know much about teleportation, but I had no idea someone could teleport to another planet.

Braydac had teleported us to the reception area of the Medical Facility. He told them I needed medical attention for a stunner blast and asked them to call Dr Aimery and Darion.

My muscles weren't as bad as they were after the prolonged stunner blast, but it was difficult to walk, so they supported me as I shuffled to one of the beds. A nurse set a Bio-scan to check my vital signs while they tried to get Braydac to lie down so they could assess and treat his wound.

He refused. "I need to speak to Dr Aimery before I go back."

The nurse looked confused. "Go back where? You won't tell us where you teleported from."

"I'll tell Dr Aimery so I don't have to keep repeating myself."

She sighed. "Okay. He's on his way."

Dr Aimery walked in with Darion following behind. "Novak? What the bloody hell's going on?" He looked at me and his eyebrows rose. "Larissa? I thought you were back on Shakira." He turned back to Braydac. "Where is Tamisan?"

"It's a long story, Doc. She's alive. I need to get her back. I managed to get Larissa back here first. She's okay but she's been stunned."

Darion stepped forward, his eyes wild. "You *bastard!* Where is she?"

Dr Aimery put an arm across Darion's chest. "Settle down, Andiyar. We need to be calm." He turned back to Braydac. "Start talking."

"Tamisan is alive. We were trying to escape and Larissa was stunned and I ported her out. Tamisan didn't follow us so we had to leave her behind, but I'll go back and get her."

"You left her behind?" Darion yelled.

Dr Aimery remained somewhat calm. "Escaped from where?"

"The planet, Korovska."

Darion stepped forward again. "What the hell? How did she end up there? What did you do to her?"

I was missing something here. Why was Darion accusing Braydac of doing something to Tamisan?

"I haven't done anything to her. The Korovskans are the enemy here, not me. I need to catch my breath and go back. The Korovskans want to carry on from where Starrick left off. That's why they grabbed Larissa from Shakira as well." All eyes turned to me. "She was his success story. Now they want to transfer Tamisan's Talent to their own people — who don't naturally possess Talent — and create an army of super soldiers. We can't let them succeed."

They were shocked into silence for a few moments. Braydac answered some more of their questions as more people piled into the room in military uniforms.

Braydac turned to the nurses. "Do you have a spare bed you can use for Tamisan?"

One of them pointed at a bed that was across from mine and two cubicles over. "Over there."

"Show me."

I was surprised they let him walk over to the bed to have a look. He looked at it and took note of the surrounding area before walking back to my bed.

The questions started again, but he put up a hand and said, "I have to go back now. I'm the only one who can bring Tamisan back." He looked directly at Darion. "I will bring her back with me."

As they protested and Darion stepped forward, he disappeared, leaving them standing there with their mouths hanging open.

They turned to me again and asked so many questions that I didn't know where to start.

I put my hands up. "Please, one at a time."

Dr Aimery gave me an apologetic smile. "I'm sorry, Larissa. We have so many unanswered questions since Braydac teleported Tamisan and another man, Nykolar Taarel, out of the jungle during a scuffle. They've been missing for nine days."

"Braydac took Tamisan to Korovska? Why? I thought he worked here. For Voyager Division."

"He does. But then he helped Nykolar avoid being arrested for trying to kill Tamisan and things got out of hand with Nykolar stunning most of the people present and Braydac teleporting the three of them away. There has been no sign of them since or any kind of message from the Korovska."

"I don't know anyone named Nykolar."

Dr Aimery frowned and exchanged a look with one of the soldiers who looked to be a commander or some similar rank — I wasn't familiar with their uniforms.

I told them what had happened to me since I'd been kidnapped from Shakira. I hoped there was a way for them to somehow stop the Korovska. Maybe if the authorities on Korovska squashed this while it was still in its early stages, they could be sure all the data had been destroyed.

I could see the concern on their faces, but Darion's was pale. It looked as if he hadn't slept much during those nine days. My heart went out to him and I hoped there wasn't going to be some devastating news for him. Surely Braydac would be able to bring Tamisan back.

If she was still in the lab, it might be difficult. He would have to wait until she was alone or back in her room. He could be gone for hours.

It was probably only about twenty minutes later when Tamisan's voice broke the silence. "Are we at Jannali?"

CHAPTER 32

I Had to Protect My Heart

"Yes," Braydac assured her.

My heart raced as everyone rushed to the bed that the nurse had pointed out to Braydac.

Darion asked her if she was okay and his broken voice almost destroyed my heart.

"Yes. It's so good to see you," she said.

I wanted to see what was happening, but didn't want to interrupt their reunion, so I peeked into the cubicle next to mine to check if it was occupied. The bed was empty and the curtain was drawn across the front of the cubicle so I crept along the curtain until I reached the other corner. From there I could see Tamisan's cubicle through a small gap in the curtain.

She was sitting up in the bed clinging to Darion while they both cried. My heart swelled and tears blurred my vision. I was so happy for them. I could feel the love they felt for each other radiating from them in waves. It was so beautiful.

This was what it felt like to be truly loved. To have someone care so deeply for you. And to care about them just as much.

I knew they weren't my feelings, but I'd gotten a taste of what that felt like when I'd been in Janssen's arms. I only hoped he'd survived so I could hold him again.

Tamisan took a deep breath. "It's okay. I'm okay. I'm back. But there's a problem. They gave me a new tracker that blocks my Talent."

Darion stroked her long hair. "We can turn it off. Braydac gave us a controller."

She pulled away from Darion and found Braydac in the crowd. "Thank you so much, Braydac. I thought I'd never get out of there."

She let out a sob, but managed to regain control.

Braydac shifted uneasily. "I... I couldn't leave them with a source of Talent."

She smiled at him through her tears. "Yeah. You keep telling yourself that."

I heard a noise behind me.

"Larissa?"

My heart leapt as I turned and looked up into those dark eyes I thought I'd never see again.

"Janssen?" I whispered.

He opened his mouth to respond, but before I could think, I'd launched myself at him and flung my arms around him.

He only hesitated for a second before responding and soon I was sobbing into his shoulder. I couldn't help it. Everything that had happened since I was last in his arms was suddenly overwhelming and I clung to him and felt the taut muscles of his back beneath his shirt and felt his warmth and his heartbeat pounding against my ear.

Once I'd regained some semblance of control, I leaned my cheek against his and whispered, "I thought you were dead."

He squeezed me tighter, then rubbed a hand on my back in a circular motion. "I came close a few times. I hid during the attack and couldn't see what was happening. I had no way of knowing if anyone had survived, but after the shooting stopped, they started searching the area, so I had to go deeper into the jungle. I lost my way for a while, but finally came back to the landing site hours later. They'd removed everything — even the shuttle. I had no idea if any of you were alive." He gave me another squeeze. "When I finally made it out of the jungle, they told me what had happened to you and that you'd gone back home. I was so glad to hear that you weren't harmed by the experiment."

"I'm glad you're okay," I whispered. I pulled away from him so I could see his face. "My apologies for running from you on the Acronis. The last thing I wanted was to hurt you, but that's exactly what I did... I was so stupid... I was afraid." I took his hand and led him back to my cubicle and we sat side-by-side on the edge of the bed. "I need to explain a few things."

It probably wasn't a good time or place to be telling him this, but I wanted him to understand. I was determined to follow the advice I'd given to Arietta.

On the way to Althar 3, I'd told him my parents had been killed in an attack on the city and about how Gran had passed away, but I needed to tell him the rest of it. It was hard to know where to start, but once I did, everything came pouring out like a dam that had burst. I told him about Grandfather and Eli. About how hard it had been to cope with the loss of my whole family and how I'd vowed not to fight. It was good to get it off my chest. I hadn't told anyone any of this, except Gran.

There was some commotion beyond the curtain and Janssen pulled it aside — enough to see Braydac being led out the door.

He turned back. "Goodbye, Tamisan. And thank you."

"Thank you for coming back for me," she said, and I could tell she meant it.

As he turned to leave, he saw me through the gap in the curtain and nodded. I nodded back. I assumed he was under arrest.

As they walked out of sight, Janssen let the curtain drop and sat back down, taking one of my hands in his and giving it a squeeze.

"I've told you about the people I've lost due to the war, but it wasn't my whole family. I can't imagine what that would be like. You have my deepest sympathies."

"Thank you." I took a deep breath. *Here goes.* "I told you about that so you could understand why I thought the only way to get through this life was to toughen up. Otherwise, I would fall to pieces and not be able to deal with everyday problems." I grasped his hand tighter, determined to let him know everything. "When you… when we got close, I panicked. I didn't know what to do. Everyone I've ever cared about has died. I couldn't let myself care for you. I had to protect my heart."

CHAPTER 33

You're So Much Stronger Than You Know

Janssen sucked in a breath. "And then I went missing."

"I didn't know that. Right from the beginning, Starrick told me I was the *only* survivor. Thinking that I'd lost you too... It tore me apart..."

The tears streamed down my face. I couldn't hold them back any longer.

He pulled me to his chest and wrapped me in a warm embrace. "It's okay. I'm here now and I'm not going anywhere. I'll be here as long as you want me." He stroked my hair. "I don't know how you got through that. You're such a strong woman."

"I don't feel strong."

"You're so much stronger than you know." He sighed. "I wish things were different. We thought we'd get the chance to be working together. To get to know one another. We would've had time to work these things through and not had the possibility of death hanging over us."

I didn't have to question how he felt about me because I could feel his emotions as if they were my own. Until that moment, I hadn't realized how useful empathy could be.

We talked for a while longer till Dr Aimery and the commander, who introduced himself as Commander Kozienko, came in to ask me more questions. I tried to answer as truthfully as possible, but I was weary and it was getting harder to concentrate.

Dr Aimery must have been able to see it in my eyes. "We'll leave you to rest and speak to you again tomorrow."

I wasn't looking forward to that, but I managed to smile. "Okay."

They said their goodbyes and were gone.

Janssen pulled me into a hug, but then a nurse came in to check on me. We jumped apart and I felt silly, then my face heated when I recognised Abbi.

She almost squealed. "'Ello, beautiful girl! 'Ow are you feeling? I can't believe this 'appened to you. Again!"

"I'm not too bad. I was stunned not long ago, but other than that..."

"Okay, love. Let's look at ya." She used a torch to check my eyes, then looked at the data from the Bio-scan. "Do you need to talk to someone this time?"

"Uh, no. I don't think so."

She looked at Janssen and smiled. "I can see you've got someone to talk to now. That's lovely." She checked a few more things in the data. "I'm so glad you two made it back 'ere safe an' sound. An' it looks like you found love too."

My cheeks burned and Janssen's blush reached from his chest to his hairline.

"Don't be embarrassed. It's a wonderful thing. Embrace it." She made a move to leave. "It all looks good, love. I'll get the doctor to come check you over, then you can go."

The relief washed over me. "Thank you."

"Bye, beautiful people."

When I was finally released from the Medical Facility, Janssen was there waiting patiently in the reception area. I couldn't help the smile that spread across my face. After everything, I hadn't lost him.

He returned my smile. "Ready to get out of here?"

"Yes!"

He put an arm around my shoulders and led me out the door. I had no idea where we were going and I didn't care as long as I was with him. Now that I'd stopped fighting my feelings, I felt a genuine attraction to him — not just a physical attraction, but something deep in my chest. There were no words to describe it.

We walked down a few hallways that all looked the same.

Janssen brought us to a halt in the middle of a hallway. "When we were due to start working here almost two months ago, we were assigned our own quarters. This," he swung his arm wide towards a door on our right, "was to be your room."

I sucked in a breath.

He stepped closer to the door. "You need to use your thumbprint to open your door."

I pressed my thumb to the lock and the door swooshed open. It seemed quite surreal. This should have happened months ago. I should have been able to move in here with excitement in my veins and plans for my new job racing through my mind.

We stepped inside. It wasn't anything fancy, with an open plan for the living, dining, and kitchen areas, and a hall leading to what I assumed were the bedroom and bathroom. I tried to imagine what it should have felt like.

What happens now? I wondered.

After all the questioning, no one had actually spelled out what would happen next. Would I have to stay here while they conducted an inquiry? Would I be called up to testify in court?

I decided to put my questions aside until tomorrow. Right now I needed to rest and find something to eat.

Janssen took my hand and led me to the kitchen area. "You must be hungry. Let's see what there is to eat."

It was like he'd read my mind, but it wouldn't have been hard to guess. I had no idea how long I'd been in the Medical Facility or how long it had been since I'd last eaten.

As he started to prepare some food, I was suddenly ravenous. He cooked some pasta and put it together with minced meat and a tomato-flavoured sauce.

My heart fluttered. Tomatoes were one of the vegetables from Earth that Janssen and I had seen that first night in the hydroponics garden. Now I'd get to taste them.

We sat down to eat and I thanked him as my mouth watered. The smell was divine. I hoped it tasted just as good.

Once I'd taken my first mouthful, I moaned. It was every bit as good as it smelled. And it was so good to eat something that wasn't a goopy unrecognisable mess.

"This is unbelievably good. Can you show me how to cook it?"

"Yes, of course. It is a dish from Earth called spaghetti bolognaise. I discovered it here on the base."

Shakirans didn't adopt many things from other cultures. After having a Taonese grandmother, I disagreed with their attitude towards other cultures and races. Losing that attitude would go a long way toward avoiding war with neighbouring planets.

Most Shakirans were too arrogant for their own good.

That made me think of home. Some of the things that Grandfather had said and done. He was all about honour and was adamant that we should never do anything that would bring shame on the family. I wondered what he would think of all of this.

I looked up and Janssen looked like he was deep in thought.

He looked at me. "My family made it a thing to go camping on the holidays when I was young, so I guess being in the jungle wasn't as hard for me as it was for poor Zhenna — I mean Tamisan."

"Yes. I used to go camping with family too, but Zhenna was freaking out about some of the crawling insects when we were looking for samples on the edge of that clearing. She must've had a very hard time."

He frowned. "Those dinosaurs were absolutely terrifying. I had to run from more than one creature and had to climb a tree or two to avoid being dinner for those big T-Rex look-alikes. There's even giant alligators in the rivers. Then you've got to avoid some of the people too — although, the Bahadori don't look like people. Those ugly monsters are cruel. The way they treat the natives they capture and put in chains..." He shook his head.

We talked for a while and Janssen finished eating and put his fork down. "What's it like? Being a Talent, I mean."

CHAPTER 34

I Never Want to Let You Go

"It was scary at first because people's thoughts were coming through to me and I thought I was going crazy. I had to be shown how to tune them all out."

"That sounds awful."

"It was, but it's okay now. I have control over that. I also had to learn how to stop myself from broadcasting some of my thoughts to other Telepaths. It was a bit embarrassing to find out I was doing that."

"Oh, yeah. I could see how that would be a problem."

"The telekinesis took a while to grasp, but it helped me — when I actually remembered to use it."

Shame washed over me when I thought of everything that happened during our escape and could see all the things I could have done using telekinesis. It would get easier to do these things over time, I was sure.

I knew Janssen would be wondering what I could do, so I concentrated on my fork and lifted it up into the air between us and the look on his face was priceless.

I made it spin around in a circle. "Put your hand out."

He put his hand out palm-up and I gently laid the fork onto it.

"Wow. That's amazing."

"It is amazing." I watched his eyes go wide. *"If you want to respond, you only have to think it in the forefront of your mind and I will see it."*

His eyes went wider. *Really?*

"Yes."

Wow.

"Don't worry. I won't read anything else from your mind. There's rules in place for all Talents. I'm not supposed to read anyone's mind without their permission. I'm not really good at it yet anyway."

He let his hand slowly drop down to the table, the fork in his grip forgotten. "You are so amazing," he breathed.

My empathic ability must have gotten stronger, or maybe I was feeling his emotions because they were so strong and were directed at me. And they mirrored my own.

I'd been loved before, but this was different. This wasn't the love of a family member.

He took one of my hands in his and kissed my fingers, one at a time. I sucked in a breath and enjoyed the sensations.

He stood suddenly and pulled me to my feet, then took me in his arms. I stared into his dark eyes for a few moments as my hands ran up his back.

He leaned his forehead against mine. "I never thought I'd get the chance to hold you again."

My breath hitched. "Me neither."

He breathed in slowly as he seemed to fight for control over his emotions and I could feel them bubbling up to the surface.

While his eyes were closed, I dared to press my lips to his. He sucked in a sharp breath and returned my kiss.

He only hesitated for a moment before kissing me again, long and slow. It was so good and I thought I'd melt into a puddle on the floor. His hands were in my hair and my hands reached up to play with the hair at the nape of his neck.

Our kisses became more urgent and I could feel myself floating away and I just let go. Nothing could make me run from the room this time. I *wanted* this feeling. I wanted to make him feel the same.

We soon had to break apart to catch our breaths and Janssen cupped my cheeks in his hands. "Wow."

The way he looked at me had my heart swelling to twice its size. I wanted him to look at me like that forever. I wanted him to hold me forever.

He held me closer. "I never want to let you go."

Closing my eyes, I soaked it up, took in his scent, the feeling of his arms around me, the feel of his muscles against my palms.

After a few minutes, he took another deep breath and rested his forehead against mine. "What are your plans? What will you do when you leave here?"

He rubbed my back and I revelled in the warm sensations. "I was planning on selling Gran's house and moving away from the area and all the memories. I was actually about to look at a new place when the Korovska kidnapped me. I even had someone coming out to see the farm. I have no idea what's happening there now. I need to contact someone on Shakira and I need to get back there."

"You still plan to continue your gran's practice of growing medicinal plants, yes?"

"Yes. I want to save lives, not take them."

"After everything you've told me, I can see why."

He continued rubbing my back as I held him close and breathed him in.

His hands stilled. "I want to help you."

My eyes flew open and I moved back so I could see his face. "How?"

"I own a second house on my parents' property. As I've told you, I came out here to study the plants on other planets to see if there was a market for them back home, or to learn ways to improve our methods of cultivation with our existing crops. I've now abandoned that idea. I'm set to take over from my parents when they retire. I think we could set you up with your own plot on the property and you could continue your research."

Tears stung my eyes. "Really? Would your parents agree to that?"

"I think they would. I have spoken to them since I was rescued from the jungle and they are still kind of in shock. They were initially told that I was dead. I can't imagine how that feels."

"I can."

He squeezed me tighter. "You have my apologies that you had to go through that. It wasn't supposed to be this way."

"It wasn't your fault."

I tried to push those memories away and focus on how I was feeling in the moment. I needed to stay positive and look to the future.

He stroked my hair. "I will check with my parents, of course, but I think we could work something out."

I hugged him tight and whispered, "Thank you."

Epilogue
A Welcoming Gift

The flowers on the dining table were beautiful, bursting from the vase with plenty of colour as they filled the room with a wonderful fragrance. I couldn't help the smile that spread across my face. Delphinas were my favourite flower with rounded petals in a brilliant shade of magenta and a deep blue centre.

"Mother wanted to make you feel at home," Janssen said as he followed me inside.

"They're amazing. I know how hard it is to get them the right shade of magenta. She must be proud."

"Yes, she is."

"I must thank her."

He smiled. "You can do that later when we go over for dinner. She'll be pleased that you like them."

Janssen's parents had been very welcoming when I'd met them on a Vid call and again in person and were enthusiastic about me moving in and continuing Gran's work; they thought Janssen's idea was perfect.

We'd stayed at Jannali for a couple of weeks until Starfleet Federation had no further need of us in their investigation and the Acronis was due to return to Earth. We'd had two more weeks to enjoy each other's company and get to know each other properly this time without my stupid fears getting in the way.

The Korovska had already been under investigation and now The Six Star Alliance and Starfleet Federation were involved. It would take a long time to investigate fully, but my main concern was stopping them creating their army. I would do everything in my power to save lives.

We'd been told that if they needed any more information, they would call us. We would need to travel to Earth when we were called as witnesses, but thankfully, it only took three days to get there from Shakira.

Dr Aimery had removed my tracker before I'd returned home and I was relieved to know that I couldn't be tracked again. He'd said that Braydac had the ability to block Talent, which was extremely rare. The fact that the Korovska had taken this ability and planned to give it to their army of super soldiers was the thing that made him turn on them and help us escape. I shuddered to think of what their army could do if they could block their enemies' Talent.

In between everything else, it had taken weeks to sort out the sale of my house. The people who were interested in the house before had moved on as I expected, but we'd eventually found a buyer.

It was now time to rest and settle into Janssen's house. I was eager to get to work on my plants and my research, but also to spend time with Janssen and see where things led us. If things didn't work out, I still had the money from the house, but, so far, I couldn't see that happening — we were so happy together.

Janssen gave me a tour of the house and after putting the kettle on to boil, held his arms out to me and I melted into them.

I sucked in a slow, deep breath and I was home.

How could I have denied myself this happiness for so long? Fear was a powerful thing and it had blinded me to the person right in front of me and to the opportunity to be truly happy and fulfilled. A feeling of peace settled over me and worked its way into my bones. I could finally relax.

Janssen's hands moved from my back to my shoulders and he ran his hands gently through my hair, making my breath hitch. As I exhaled, I pulled him closer. His muscular back felt good under my fingers and he moved his head down until his lips were inches from my neck and stopped. I held my breath. He pressed his lips to my skin and I sucked in a sharp breath, taking in every sensation running through me.

He trailed kisses down to my shoulder, back up and along my jaw, and finally to my lips where he lit a fire. I returned his kisses with an urgency that shocked me. I was melting on the spot and trying to pull him closer. I couldn't get enough of him and the whirlwind of feelings threatening to sweep me away. He deepened the kiss and I was losing control.

He pulled away so we could catch our breaths and we stood holding each other. Each time I kissed him seemed to be better than the last, which I didn't think was possible.

He pulled back and looked into my eyes. "I know it's early days yet, but if things keep progressing the way they are, I am confident that we will form a life bond."

Tears stung my eyes as I nodded. "I feel the same way."

"We will take things as they come."

He moved away from me and reached into the cutlery drawer, presumably to take out some spoons, but instead he found a small white box.

"I couldn't buy this myself because we were in deep space, so Mother helped me. It was hard to find — most of the designs were a weapon of some kind and I knew you wouldn't want that." He placed the box on my palm. "This is a welcoming gift."

My heart fluttered in my chest as I slowly raised the lid. Resting inside on a plush blue cushion was a silver chain with a pendant in the shape of a Delphina, with a blue gemstone in the centre to match the blue centre of the flower.

I gasped.

"It's beautiful," I breathed.

"*You* are beautiful."

I looked into his dark eyes and smiled. "Thank you."

"It's my pleasure, my love."

I closed the box and flung my arms around him. "I love you."

"I love you too, my darling."

⸻ ❖ ⸻

This is the end of this story, but not the end of this book. Keep reading for some extra goodies:
An excerpt from the first book in the *Lightning Touch Series*,
TOUCH OF LIGHTNING
An offer of a free book
Acknowledgements
A list of other books by Susan McKenzie
About the author

⸻ ❖ ⸻

Did you enjoy this book?
Help the next reader to enjoy it too.
Reviews are such a fantastic way for people to express the way a book made them feel. A way to share it with the world.

Indie authors don't have the huge budgets that the big New
York publishers have, but we have something more powerful.
We have loyal readers like you.
It would be so awesome if you could share what you thought of
this book by leaving a review on the site where you purchased
it.
Thank you so much.
Sue

Keep reading for an excerpt from the first book in the *Lightning
Touch Series,* ***TOUCH OF LIGHTNING***

Excerpt: Touch of Lightning (Lightning Touch Book 1)

Chapter 1: (Not) Good Vibrations

The screen on the Navigational Computer flashed red in the top right corner and my heart stuttered. It would've taken a fraction of a second to bring up the following warning message, but to me, it felt like minutes.

No...

This was the part of my job that I hated.

There was ground movement predicted in the area. *Strong* ground movement. They estimated a 4.5 on the meter, complete with aftershocks.

"Javolo?" My heart was pounding in my throat and I could hardly push the word out.

"Yeah?" His voice sounded extra scratchy over the Com system today.

I could feel a cold sweat forming on my forehead. "You need to hang on to something. You're about to get a four point five."

"Okay, Cal. Will do."

Another thing I couldn't stand was the wait. I couldn't breathe properly. I tried to sit still in my seat and calm down. It didn't work. It *never* worked. If they knew how badly the quakes affected me, I'd lose my job instantly.

Breathe... Just breathe. In. Out. In. Out.

My hands were shaking so badly that I shoved them under my thighs to stop them.

"Are you somewhere relatively safe?" I could hear the tremor in my voice and hoped the distortion through the Com would hide it.

"Yep."

I resisted the urge to ask Javolo if he felt anything yet. I couldn't ask any questions that could give away how I was really feeling. I had to appear calm. They recorded *all* conversations.

In. Out. Relax...

I wasn't scared for me. I was safe and sound in my little cubicle up on the space station while Javolo was underground down on the planet, Kronos, mining the universe's most sort-after mineral, Amakio, and putting his life on the line. I was scared for *him*, and all of the other Diggers down there.

Most of the quakes on the planet were minor, and there had only been one partial collapse of one of the tunnels since I'd started working for Katoa Intergalactic Mining and Exploration five months before, but that knowledge didn't help to ease my panic every time it happened.

"Okay, here it comes..."

My heart stopped, I was sure of it. Then galloped ahead full speed as I waited.

Breathe. In. Out. In. Out. Relax... Let go of the desk... Relax... Start with your fingers and toes...

I kept trying to relax, one part of me at a time. Maybe it helped. I couldn't tell.

Why did I even apply for this job in the first place? Yeah, I know. I gotta start somewhere and work my way up... But I don't think I can handle this. Panicking every time I see those words on the screen... I couldn't cope if something happened to Javolo... He's my friend... My best friend.

Sure, there were the girls I knew from work — the other Nav Operators and admin staff — but it was different with them. They were friends, but not *real* friends. I couldn't really talk to them. Not about the important stuff.

Then there was Malvolio. We'd been seeing each other for about four weeks, but that was a totally different kind of relationship.

"Cal?"

Javolo's voice brought my thoughts back to the present. "Uh, yeah?"

Only Javolo would think to shorten my surname from Callista to Cal, as if it was my first name.

He reported exactly what the Nav Computer had told me as it happened. Three smaller tremors... Then...

"Whoah!"

I put my hand over my mouth so I wouldn't cry out. Then I started my relaxation techniques again. I had to pull myself together, and quickly. I had to wipe the image of being surrounded by dirt and tree roots from my mind.

"Okay. It's gone."

I remembered to remove my hand. I took a deep breath and opened my mouth to talk, but Javolo beat me to it.

"That was a big one. Nearly knocked me on my butt."

A picture of him falling onto his butt in his cumbersome Mech-suit popped into my mind. Now *that* would be funny to see. And it would be even funnier once he tried to get back up. I'd seen footage of just how difficult that task was in a training video.

Mech-suits were big mechanical suits that the Diggers could climb into that supplied oxygen and boosted their strength so they could dig up the Amakio and bring it back to the waiting shuttles. They had arms and legs powered by hydraulics that were extensions of the Diggers limbs, allowing them to dig and lift heavy weights while mining.

"I *told* you to hang on to something."

There really wasn't anything he could hold on to down there, but I had to say something to try to lighten the situation.

I forced myself to breathe slower and waited for my heartbeat to return to normal. My hands still shook so I clasped them together in my lap. I hated feeling like this. It was overwhelming, but I was thankful he was okay.

"Yeah, that you did..." he said.

I braced myself and waited for more aftershocks. They were only minor. I had to keep telling myself everything was okay and to relax.

I pulled my thoughts from the images in my mind that I wish I could forget and I tried to keep my voice even. "Okay, report."

"No damage. No more ground movement. The suit's reporting that all systems are functioning normally. Anyway, guess what?"

I smiled. Javolo didn't miss a beat. It was straight back to our conversation. "What?"

I busied myself with the Nav Computer terminal, collating all the information that Javolo's Mech-suit had reported before the quake so it could correlate with the sixteen orbiting navigational satellites and make the necessary corrections to his position on the screen. Now I had his exact location.

"Last night I saw the most beautiful woman I've ever seen!" he exclaimed through the static over the Com.

Where did that come from? I wondered.

The last thing we were talking about that wasn't work-related was a HoloMovie I'd seen recently about a droid that thought it was human. But I couldn't pass up an opportunity to tease him.

"Ah-huh. Like the redhead you saw last month?" I laughed. "Or the brunette in the grav shaft last week?"

"No," he said quickly, "this is different. Cut me some slack, huh?"

"Nah. Can't do that." I giggled. I couldn't help myself. I didn't care that I was sitting in my dull little cubicle all by myself with a wide grin plastered on my face.

This was the part of the job I loved the most. I could dig at him like that and he knew I was kidding. He may have been my work partner, but it wasn't all business. We could joke around and be ourselves, even though it was frowned upon by 'The Company' as we called it.

"She looked amazing," he continued.

I rolled my eyes and stopped myself from laughing out loud. "*Suuure* she did."

I couldn't *agree* with him. What would be the fun in that?

"I'm serious."

The Nav Computer was taking its sweet time. We couldn't do anything until I had all of the information. There could be warnings in the last few segments of data.

My mind wandered while we waited. Rogan, the partner I'd had before Javolo, was all business and no interesting conversation. Once he'd been replaced by Javolo, my job had become a lot more interesting. A lot more fun.

I looked back at the data on the screen. Still not finished. Talk about slow. It was frustrating. Everything was so out-dated and archaic here. They needed to update the whole system and I knew exactly which one would be able to handle the workload. Computers were something I knew well. Something I'd excelled in throughout my schooling.

I'd majored in Polymer Science and Engineering and wanted to work for Katoa's research department on things like improving the materials for the Mech-suits and oxygen masks, but I'd quickly realised once I'd started working here that they weren't interested in keeping their technology up-to-date. It seemed they didn't like to spend money, even if it would improve efficiency and safety. I only had to look at the ridiculously archaic equipment we were forced to work with to see that. Typical. Were all large companies like this?

I seriously hoped not.

This low-end job was supposed to be my start so I could move up to Research and Development, but I'd decided on a different strategy. I'd already started to research other companies. There was no way I was going to stay here once my two-year contract was up. It had turned out to be a dead-end job, even if it was with one of the biggest companies in the Known Universe.

"Where to now, Boss?"

I tried to suppress a giggle, and failed. "Ah, I like that."

"Like what?"

I sat up straighter. "You admitting I'm the boss."

"Well, you order me around all day and I have to obey your every command. It's almost like we're married."

Chapter 2: Why Do I Feel Like This?

I stopped what I was doing. Why did my stomach do a little fluttery dance when he said that?

I tried to concentrate on what I was supposed to do next. "Umm, still waiting on the computer to give me everything."

Then the last of the information finally hit the screen. I read through all the relevant stuff. No warnings. No problems.

Good.

"No probs with the report. Time to get back to work."

"Yes, Ma'am."

I checked the blurb on the side of the screen telling me where the next vein started. "Head down the tunnel to your right."

"On it."

I remembered what we were talking about. "Come on then, tell me about her."

"She has long dark hair and bright blue eyes that seem to flash at you when she smiles," he began.

Oh, wow... What a description! I thought, a smile tugging at my lips. Javolo was such a romantic.

"Turn left at that intersection and go down about twenty metres," I said. I could hear the suit's hydraulics as he walked the distance. That was unusual. The connection was clearer than normal for a few seconds.

"And she has the most perfect bod..."

Typical male, I laughed to myself. So much for being a romantic. "Yeah, I believe you..." I told him. "Stop there."

"It's true," he protested. "Okay, it's true *this* time... Well, ya know, last time the girl wasn't perfect like I'd said, but still really pretty. And a really nice person... and married."

And not even human. Not that he would've had a problem with that — but it was funny that Javolo had thought she was. I guess her tail would've been hidden under her dress. I giggled. "Now go forward. Bit more... Bit more. Stop. Turn to your right. You should be facing a wall with a visible vein through it."

"Yep."

"Okay, start. Middle of the road."

"Yes, Ma'am."

He immediately started up his rock-breaker, which was attached to the left arm of his Mech-suit. The other arm sported a four-pronged mechanical hand for picking up samples, with a shovel-like scoop on the back of its "wrist" for scooping the debris away. The mechanical hand and other parts of the suit contained sensors that detected traces of Amakio and transmitted the locations to the Nav Computer. This information was triangulated with data from the other Diggers and the sixteen satellites to pinpoint the mineral deposits under the ground.

While Javolo worked, it was too noisy for us to talk, so I twirled a piece of my long hair around my finger as I watched the screen to check for any new data or warnings, and was left to my thoughts. More and more often lately, my thoughts came back to the end of our partnership — our Rotation — together and I couldn't help feeling anxious about it.

The contract with Katoa was for two years. They divided the time up into four Rotations of six months each. We worked with one partner for six months, then, so we didn't get too attached, we were assigned a different one for each Rotation. This was my first Rotation, and after a short stint with Rogan, I'd been paired with Javolo. Javolo and I only had about a month left before we were assigned new partners. Maybe we *were* too close according to the company's guidelines, but we were just friends. Really good friends. I felt a sense of loss at the thought of never being able to talk to him every day, and I hadn't even experienced the loss yet. It was weird. And really awful.

Why do I feel like this? I thought as my fingernails tapped the grey desk. I had no answer. *Why do we have to part ways? And why is this cubicle so drab and grey? It's enough to make anyone depressed.*

I thought about who I might end up working with. What if it was someone I didn't like, or someone like Rogan that didn't share my sense of humour? The chances of being part-nered with someone with the same sense of humour and/or the same interests were pretty slim. That wasn't a very encouraging thought.

Who would I be working with after next month? If we didn't get along, I'd be stuck with him — or her — for *six months*. That would make my job difficult. It would make my life miserable. Of course, it was my job and I'd suck it up and do it, but I wished I could keep things the way they were.

I pushed all that aside for now.

I thought about what I might do on my next rostered day off. Maybe go swimming. It was always refreshing and it helped me to clear my mind so I could think and reflect. Something about water had always made me feel calm and relaxed. Or I could take a long walk in the park near my apartment. That was always good for my soul. I loved to lie on the grass and watch the birds flitting amongst the trees.

Those pleasant images were replaced by images of Malvolio's angry face the night before at dinner when the waitress brought him a "slightly cold" meal. I couldn't believe how angry he'd been over something so trivial...

Chapter 3: Nothing But the Best for My Girl

I couldn't think about Malvolio now. I had to concentrate on work. I tucked those thoughts away for later and thought about the park again.

After a few more minutes of noisy rock-breaking, Javolo began scooping out the rubble from the hole he'd created. "I can see the rest of the vein. It goes off to the right. Just need to collect this lot first."

"Okay."

I felt myself relax a little. I needed to concentrate on the job at hand.

I encouraged him to tell me what he could remember of the 'perfect' woman and it turned out that he'd only seen her for a brief moment as the door to the grav shaft slid shut near the entrance to the Golden Palace restaurant.

I gasped when I heard the name. The restaurant stood on the border between the Diggers' Section and the rest of Perseus Station and was divided into two separate establishments. One for the Diggers and one for the rest of the space station. I'd been there the night before with Malvolio in the main section where he'd had his little tantrum. Javolo had obviously been in the Diggers' Section.

A strange feeling crept over my skin as I thought about the fact that we'd been within fifty metres of each other and neither of us knew it. The sad part was that even if we'd come face-to-face, we wouldn't have recognised each other. Diggers and Navs lived in separate sections of the space station and were never allowed to meet. That way they couldn't get personally involved and it couldn't affect their job performance. I had no idea what Javolo looked like.

I tried to shrug off the feeling.

I was amazed that Javolo could give me so many details about the girl after such a quick glance, and I suspected his mind had filled in some of the blanks. If he saw her again, it would be a different story. Maybe her eyes weren't even blue, but I loved his poetic description of them.

It took Javolo the rest of the morning to extract the Amakio from that location, having to make more than one trip with his floating tub in tow. I was always amused when imagining the floating rectangular tub harnessed to the Mech-suit, hovering along behind him at mid-thigh level wherever he went. I'd seen them on the training videos. It was a strange sight.

My mind wandered again. It was almost time for lunch and I had to force myself to stop thinking about food and focus.

"Hey, Cal, how's What's-his-name goin'?" Javolo asked.

A weird sensation flowed through me at the question, like all the air had left my lungs, but I responded automatically. "It's not *What's-his-name* — it's Malvolio."

I heard him snicker. "What kind of name is Malvolio anyway?" he jeered. "Do you call him Mal for short, or just Vol?"

Of course, Javolo couldn't pass up an opportunity to tease me about him.

"No," I answered flatly. "Neither. He wouldn't appreciate his name shortened like that." I tried to imagine Malvolio's reaction if I called him either of those names. A cringe. Or maybe an eye roll. But I didn't want to be thinking about him right now.

"Oh, too good for the good ol' nickname, 'ey?"

"Lay off him," I warned. "He's a nice guy."

I grimaced inwardly and frowned. He was far from nice last night. That poor waitress.

How did things change so much? He was such a gentleman when we'd met. He'd somehow managed to make me break my promise to myself that I wouldn't get involved with anyone while I was working here.

I wasn't sure what to do or what I'd say when I saw him. I would have to deal with that later. Right now, we had work to do.

The Nav Computer spewed out our next location. "Okay, we have our next place…"

I'd just sat down at an empty table with my lunch when I heard a familiar voice.

"Lennina, darling. How are you?"

My stomach dropped and I looked up to see Malvolio smiling at me. I forced a smile onto my face. "Oh, hi."

That's not the reaction I should have felt. I should be happy to see him. What was wrong with me?

He sat across from me and grabbed one of my hands in both of his. I felt something small and rectangular against my palm and turned my hand over to find a small gift box.

"Oh! Um, thank you!"

I didn't know what to say. He never listened when I told him not to buy me gifts all the time. It was nice to receive them, but I didn't feel comfortable when he spent so much money on me.

"Well, aren't you going to open it?"

I sucked in a breath. Why was I just staring at it? I pulled the tiny ribbon and opened the box to find a sparkling pair of diamond earrings sitting neatly inside. "Oh, wow… They're beautiful…"

I was lost for words. They *were* beautiful. And expensive. Something I could never afford. I had to keep reminding myself that he had a high-credit position as the MIC of a company called Galaxy Mech, the company that made the Mech-suits for Katoa, and he probably didn't consider them to be expensive.

I didn't think I'd ever get used to receiving such expensive things.

I looked up at him again. He was smiling and his grey eyes were so intense. He was good looking in a sophisticated sort of way and I knew all the women drooled over him. It felt good knowing he was mine and that they were jealous.

"Nothing but the best for my girl," he said. When I didn't respond, he said, "Aren't you going to put them on?"

"Um. I thought it would be better if I waited till I got home."

He frowned. "Why? Don't you like them?"

"Yes, of course I do. It's just…"

"Just what?"

"I'm at work."

"And?"

"I don't want anything to happen to them. They're too expensive. I don't want to lose them."

"You'll be sitting in an office in front of a computer. How could anything happen to them?"

I squirmed in my seat. How could I explain? I wasn't even sure I understood what I was thinking. "Uh, I just don't think I should—"

"You don't want them, is that it?"

"No! I didn't say that."

"You didn't have to. Actions speak louder than words." He rubbed his jaw for a few seconds. "Who is he?"

***

TOUCH OF LIGHTNING (*Lightning Touch Book 1*) is available right now. Use the QR Code to grab your copy!

Or type this into your browser: https://books2read.com/touch-of-lightning

***

Keep reading for a chance to sign up for a free novelette, **THE ALIEN**

ACKNOWLEDGEMENTS

Writing a book is hard, and usually, it's a solitary undertaking. But recently, I've asked beta readers to give me honest feedback before the book is released, which helps me to shape the story into something better. Fresh eyes looking at my words from different points of view. I've learned a lot and I am forever grateful to them for taking the time to give me their honest opinions. Thank you, Kimberly Rodighiero and Wanda Bradford for your contributions to this book.

I found a small group of authors a few years back that understand what it's like and help me along my journey. I'd like to thank them personally. They are Angharad Thompson Rees, Bill Duncan, Catherine Lee, Rachel Sanderson, Megan Daymond, and Sam Gee — members of the 10K Readers + SPF – Sydney Meet Up group. I don't know where I'd be without you.

My parents have always told me I could do anything if I put my mind to it and my family support me in everything I do, especially with my writing. I love you all.

I'd like to thank all of the members of the Sydney Shadows Club who have supported me. I am honoured to be a member of the club.

Lastly, to Pete, for sharing your life with me and for being my biggest supporter, alpha reader and proofreader. (And music

teacher.) It's so helpful to be able to run ideas by you and see
what you think — even before I start writing — something I've
never had before. I can't thank you enough for all that you do.
I love you.

Books by Susan McKenzie

THE JADORI SERIES (ONGOING SERIES):
Fire and Magic is being released in a serialized format (1 chapter per week) on reamstories.com right now!

***

THE TAMISAN SERIES (COMPLETED SERIES):
Tamisan

Enigma

A Tamisan Novella – Shakiran: Larissa's Story

***

THE LIGHTNING TOUCH SERIES (COMPLETED SERIES):
Touch of Lightning
Power of Lightning

Just remember, a completed series means you can binge read the whole series now — no waiting for the next book to release.

About the Author

Susan McKenzie is an Australian author who loves creating worlds of fantasy and science fiction with fascinating characters and slow-burn low-spice romance.

Her books are full of interesting and relatable characters who use their psychic abilities or magical powers to fight their way out of trouble.

She loves stories that hit you in the feels.

She's not a typical author coffee addict - but chocolate? Now that's a different story. When she's not writing, she loves to paint, draw, sing, and play the guitar.

Get in touch with Sue.
Follow Sue on her Ream site for early access and bonus/deleted scenes:
https://reamstories.com/susanmckenzie
Follow Sue on her Amazon author page:
amazon.com/author/susancarter
Visit Sue's website:
http://susanmckenzieauthor.com

Follow Sue on Facebook:
https://www.facebook.com/SueMcKenzieAuthor